Codename: Starman

Book 1

The Kalashnikov Kiss

Books by Mack Maloney

Mack Maloney's Haunted Universe
Iron Star
Thunder Alley

Starhawk *series*
Starhawk
Planet America
The Fourth Empire
Battle at Zero Point
Storm Over Saturn

Chopper Ops *series*
Chopper Ops
Zero Red
Shuttle Down

Strikemasters *series*
Strikemasters
Rogue War
Fulcrum

Storm Birds *series*
Desert Lightning
Thunder from Heaven
The Gathering Storm

Codename: Starman

Book 1

The Kalashnikov Kiss

Mack Maloney

SPEAKING VOLUMES, LLC
NAPLES, FLORIDA
2019

The Kalashnikov Kiss

Copyright © 2019 by Brian Kelleher

ISBN 978-1-64540-113-1

For my pal, Ross Sharp

Book One

The Kalashnikov Kiss

Chapter One

San Diego

"I'm sorry, I just can't marry you . . ."

Chris Starr opened his eyes. Morning was spilling into the vast bedroom. He turned over and yawned. She was beside him, bathed in sunshine while he was still in shadow.

Her eyes were getting teary. She was looking up at the ceiling. "I love you, but I just can't . . ."

Starr stretched and yawned again.

Angel . . .

She was gorgeous and sweet, and he loved her, too. But they'd had this conversation almost every day for the past six months. In his worst moments, he wondered if he was just a pair of ears to her.

He prayed hard for the phone to ring—and it did.

It was a voice message from his boss, slightly garbled. "The most beautiful . . . girl in San Diego is DOA . . . Marine may be involved. Download my notes. Do a canvass. Then meet me at Funny Bones 0900."

Starr leapt out of bed, saved by the bell. "Damn, work again . . ."

He went into Angel's massive wardrobe closet, stepped between two wool coats . . . and was suddenly in his own apartment.

This was the wormhole. He'd built it himself, quietly, preferring not to bother the lease company with his renovation plans. He and Angel lived in adjoining apartments at The Park 12 on Imperial Avenue. They didn't want any scandals and neither of their employers would be pleased with a cohabitation situation.

Thus, the wormhole.

Ten minutes later he reappeared in Angel's bedroom. Fresh work clothes, new ball cap, a quick shine on his boots. Both his weapons were cleaned and loaded.

Angel had pulled her sheet down, but remained curled up on the bed. Now the sunny room resembled a Playboy photoshoot. She was a professional model—and with her wholesome looks and strawberry blond hair—was always in high demand. She usually made more in a day than he did in a month—but money was never an issue with them. They were both 25 and they *really* wanted to get married.

But there was this one little hangup . . .

He leaned over and kissed her goodbye.

"Please be careful today," she told him, slow to let him go.

"You too. No falling off the catwalk."

But she stayed serious. "And can we talk about this tonight?"

"Absolutely."

He kissed her again and headed for the door.

"And you'll consult your crystal ball?" she called after him. "And ask for some kind of guidance?"

He opened the door to go. "You know it doesn't work like that."

She sighed dramatically. "Oh right, shrinkage—"

He stuck his head back in the door and said. "But I *knew* you were going to say *that*."

Chapter Two

Starr was in the Navy.

Five foot nine, blond and handsome, he'd graduated from Annapolis two years before, hoping to fly jets off aircraft carriers. But then a routine psych test showed he possessed about thirty percent more ESP than the average person. It wasn't a surprise. He'd known all his life that something was up. But now it'd been quantified by the Navy.

Three months and many more tests later, he was jump-commissioned a first lieutenant and assigned to the Naval Intelligence Law Enforcement division in San Diego, also known as NILE/West.

He'd been here ever since.

He was not a superhero. His type of ESP was called STPA2—short-term partially advanced precognitive ability. He rarely saw events in the far future. Instead he sometimes foresaw what was going to happen just a couple seconds before it happened. In Navy vernacular: "pre-cog shrinkage."

It was a blessing/curse. He knew when a bad guy was going to throw a punch; he knew when a high-speed car chase was about to go wrong. In the first instance, there was never enough time to do anything but duck. But in the second, going 80 mph on the streets of downtown or 120 up on the freeway, guns blazing, being two heartbeats ahead of everyone else could make a big difference.

*****

People knew NCIS, but who knew NILE? It was probably the least recognized acronym in the U.S. Navy.

NILE got cases NCIS couldn't take for what the Navy called "derivative environments," military-speak for unusual circumstances. Hidden way in the back of Building 4, East Section of the vast San Diego naval shipyard, Starr's office held just five people. They were listed on the building directory as the Naval Information Section, but everyone called them the X-Files guys.

Starr *had* dealt with some strange cases in his young career. Weird things happened all the time in this world, but you couldn't allow them to muck up the process. Sherlock Holmes once said, after all the crazy stuff had been eliminated, whatever remained *had* to be the truth.

Starr was a big fan of Holmes; that's another reason why he had a near 100% solve rate. The best in NILE— ever.

So, he was very good at what he did. Yet his own, romantic conundrum seemed devoid of resolution.

The problem was "Angel."

It was not her real name. Her real name was Star; last name: Kleinpeter-Morosi. She'd been trying to escape that hyphenated monster since preschool, so keeping her maiden name in marriage was not an option.

But she didn't want to be known as Star Starr.

Chapter Three

The crime scene was the Oceanside Motor Inn, an hourly place on the seediest stretch of Harbor Drive, just south of the Navy base.

Starr pulled into the parking lot at 06:15. He was driving his 1989 Jaguar XJS coupe. Five speeds, fuel-injected, 12-cylinders, armored body and bullet-proof glass. He'd recently asked the higher ups if he could install a remote controlled gun mount under the driver's side headlight. He'd been in a number of high-speed shootouts already and disabling a fleeing felon's vehicle would be a lot easier if he had a weapon sticking out of the hood.

But the Navy said no.

As usual, the San Diego police had gone overboard with the yellow tape. The dreary motel was festooned with it, flapping in the breeze. Though still early morning, a small crowd had gathered. Five cops on the perimeter were keeping them back.

Starr carefully parked the Jag and then flashed his NILE badge to the uniforms.

"Room 13G," one told him. "Follow the tape."

Up the stairs, across the open balcony, he found the room filled with more SDPD, walking around, doing little. The victim was spread eagle across a heart-shaped bed, face down, a sheet tossed over the naked body.

Starr took a quick peek underneath. Early twenties. Asian. Very pretty face. There were faint ligature marks on the neck. But that was it. Whatever happened, it was quick.

A cop sidled up to him.

"Beautiful, even in death . . ." he said.

Starr couldn't disagree. He put the sheet back down and sought out the ranking SDPD officer, a captain.

"The old broad working the night desk saw a Marine leave here prior to the DOA being discovered," the cop told him, consulting his notes. "She said the guy was in a Corps day uniform and that he looked distraught."

Distraught . . .

Starr's antennas went up. He walked back out to the open balcony. The small crowd was still in the parking lot. The local media had arrived as well.

He scanned the crowd. Twenty-two people and they all moved the same way—except for one. On the periphery. Standing alone. White male, early 40s. Close-cropped hair. Arm tats. In good shape.

Wearing civilian clothes, but undoubtedly a Marine.

And, he looked distraught.

The man averted his eyes as soon as Starr locked on to him.

Then he began to run.

Chapter Four

Starr flew down the stairs, fighting yellow tape all the way. He reached the parking lot to see the suspect in full stride running south on Harborside.

He jumped into the Jag and was off. Pulling out onto Harborside, he double shifted up to fourth and buried the gas. But in those few seconds, the fleeing man had commandeered a motorcycle. He was now tearing down Harborside in excess of 100 mph. After five blocks of weaving in and out of the morning traffic, he made a sharp left turn and disappeared down Water Street.

The Jag was a great car for a chase, and soon Starr was just a half block behind him.

Then suddenly . . . *hit the brakes!*

Starr obeyed. Two seconds later an early bird school bus pulled out in front of him, coming from the right. Starr veered left into the oncoming traffic, missing a collision by inches. Tires burning and down into third, he rocketed past the school bus. The kids on board cheered as he went by.

By this time the suspect had crashed the motorcycle. Coating the intersection of Bridge and Water streets with gasoline, the bike's wreckage caught fire and the flames quickly spread. Traffic screeched to a halt.

Avoiding the blaze, the suspect carjacked a Ford SUV and was off again, now heading west.

But Starr drove right through the flames. When the fleeing man looked in his rearview mirror, he saw the Jag on his bumper and Starr pointing a Glock 9MM right at him. The man panicked and missed a turn. The SUV went up on the sidewalk, plowing into the front of a wine shop. The crash sounded like a bomb going off; broken wine splattered like blood. The SUV was destroyed, but the suspect managed to escape a second time and began running again. Now he was heading north on Wharf Street.

Starr careened onto Wharf. There was a dock at the far end crowded with tourists waiting for an excursion of the harbor. Beyond the dock was a slowly moving ferry. Beyond that was the sea.

The suspect was running wildly through the crowd, pushing people aside, knocking some to the ground. Starr squealed to a stop and began chasing him on foot, waving his Glock over his head. He was soon right behind the perp and gaining. But they were coming to the end of the pier.

Just as Starr went to grab him, the suspect took a mighty leap and flew off the dock. Arms flapping, legs flailing, he landed on the slow moving ferry with a crunch.

Starr went right after him, hurling across the expanse of water and hitting the ferry deck with an even louder crunch.

A crewman helped him to his feet, but then yelled at him over the boat's engine: "What the fuck are you guys doing, man?"

"I'm law enforcement," Starr replied, catching his breath. "He's a felon. I can't let him get away . . ."

The crewman just laughed. He yelled: "But this ferry's coming in!"

Starr barely heard him. He shouted back: "Don't let anyone off this vessel!"

Then he resumed the chase.

Along the passenger rail, up to the concourse and then down to the bottom deck, in and out of all kinds of vehicles and people, Starr and the fleeing man played a game of hide and seek while running at full speed.

Then . . . *hang on!*

A tremendous bang came from the front of the ferry; they'd hit something. Starr was slammed against the hull, but because of the last second warning, he took the blow with his shoulder and not his chin. But it still hurt like a mother.

In reality, the ferry had simply reached the dock, a hasty arrival in light of things. People were scrambling to get off, trying to get away from the two maniacs chasing each other onboard. Starr stumbled up to the passenger deck just in time to see the suspect disappear into the fleeing crowd.

He started running again, only to slam into the same crew member who'd greeted him on arrival.

"I told you not to let anyone off!" Starr yelled at him.

The man yelled right back. "You're playing Batman and I'm supposed to listen to you?"

The suspect broke away from the crowd and ran towards another pier, this one on West Ferry Road.

It housed a seaplane company—and lucky for him, he knew how to fly. But when he looked over his shoulder, he was shocked to see Starr was right on his tail again, not 50 feet behind. Reaching the end of the dock, he jumped into a plane's open cockpit, quick started the engine and began moving out into the bay. He even waved goodbye to Starr.

But Starr never stopped running. He made another impossibly acrobatic leap—leaving the dock and slamming into the plane's right-side pontoon.

That was all it took. The plane went on its side causing the propeller to hit the water. The suspect bailed out, nearly getting sliced by the flying prop shards. He immediately began swimming back towards the pier.

Starr dove deep under to avoid getting slashed. When he surfaced, he saw the perp climb back onto the dock and start running again, now heading east.

Starr swam like hell, scrambled up the dock's ladder and was in pursuit once again.

He reached the corner of Central and Vine just in time to see the suspect step onto a city bus.

The man somehow paid his fee, was ignored by the driver for being soaking wet, and took a seat by an open window at the back.

He settled in, tried to catch his breath and act normal. But then he looked to his right and saw Starr hanging on to the bus with one hand and thrusting the fist of his other through the window, clocking him.

He was out before he hit the floor.

Chapter Five

It took three cups of ice water splashed in his face before the suspect came to again.

Starr was standing over him, Glock in one hand, a cup with more ice water in the other.

They were in a special holding cell at SDPD central booking on North Harborside. The suspect was handcuffed to the bunk which in turn was locked in cement. Above the bunk was a long thin window with steel-grid reinforcing. A single dim ceiling light was swinging in some phantom breeze. The place smelled of *Clorox*, urine and cigarettes.

The suspect was a big guy. At least 6'1" and ripped; his tats featured many shooting guns and no less than three Marine Corps emblems. But when he tried to sit up, he couldn't. The chain linking the handcuffs to the bunk was too short.

"Why did you run?" Starr asked him, ready to douse him again. "Why did you make me chase you?"

The man sighed deeply. "Captain Kyle Harvey, U.S. Marine Corps. Serial number 334181391."

"You think you're a POW?"

"Captain Kyle Harvey, U.S. Marine Corps. Serial number 334181391," was the reply.

Starr typed the name into his phone—but it took a while to respond. His phone was old and not very smart. Several awkward moments passed until it finally accessed the Navy's personnel ID database. Harvey was attached to the USS *Lawrence Stone*, a guided missile cruiser being overhauled at the San Diego shipyard. It had been in port four months, part of a two-year refit.

Starr put the barrel of his Glock on the marine's nose.

"Why did you kill that girl?"

"Captain Kyle Harvey, U.S. Marine Corps. Serial number 334181391 . . ."

"Why did you go back to the motel?"

"Captain Kyle Harvey, U.S. Marine Corps. Serial number 334181391 . . ."

"Do you want a lawyer?"

"Captain Kyle Harvey, U.S. Marine Corps. Serial number 334181391 . . ."

Starr put his gun away.

"Okay, have it your way," he said, finally throwing the ice water at him. Then he took a quick sniff and added: "Enjoy your stay."

Chapter Six

Funny Bones was slang for the city's morgue.

Just a short drive from the SDPD central booking, it was not Starr's favorite place. Too many bad vibes. Too many ghosts.

But orders were orders. The motel murder victim's body had already been transported there. Starr arrived at precisely 0900, his clothes almost dry.

His boss was waiting out front. He was Navy Commander Juan Parades. A huge, darkly handsome man, he'd played linebacker at the Naval Academy for four years. Mid-40s now, twice divorced and chronically broke, he was, nevertheless, a thorough investigator and a respected officer. He also had a temper and could intimidate friends and foes alike. Everyone called him Bull.

They walked into the morgue together.

"This might be a tough one . . ." Starr said, trying to shake off his uneasiness.

"Why say that?" Bull asked.

"The vic was so . . . beautiful. You said it yourself."

Bull stopped him in his tracks. "What are you talking about?"

Starr was confused. "A hot chick gets murdered? That has an effect on me."

Bull laughed and started walking again. "I hope you're an Aerosmith fan, lieutenant," he said.

The morgue attendant was waiting for them. He pulled out the drawer holding the naked murder victim lying face up—and gasped.

So did Starr.

Yes, some outstanding cosmetic work had been done at some point—but the body was definitely not a female.

"The dude looks like a lady," Bull said to Starr. "How didn't you know?"

Starr used his dumb phone to retrieve a voice-to-text of Bull's original message. Sure enough it actually said: "The most beautiful *T-girl* in San Diego . . ."

Bull growled at him: "Get rid of that piece of shit phone. That's an order."

They retreated to the morgue's break room.

"As soon as DC learned we had a tranny on the slab, they declared it a hate crime," Bull told him. "That's why we caught the case."

"Fuck, no . . . ." Starr groaned.

"Fuck yes," Bull replied. "Our orders are to secure enough evidence to build a bias-motivated felony against our jarhead friend and get him life at hard labor, nothing less."

Starr rubbed his eyes; the saltwater had made them itchy. Hate crimes involved lots of paperwork, most of it unnecessary. DC would want tons of files, folders and written testimony sent their way—in quadruplicate. Just transmitting it all was more than could be handled by the one tech they could appropriate from the pool.

"Who's going to do all the typing?" he asked Bull wearily.

"Leave the typing to me," the boss replied. He started reading from his notes: "I have the vic as 'Mary Contrary.' Transgender. Bartender. Illegal. Originally from Manila. Died of a broken neck, delivered with one learned twist, I suspect."

It was Starr's turn. "The perp is Captain Kyle Harvey, U.S. Marine Corps. Serial number 334181391. Security officer for the USS *Stone*, guided missile cruiser here for a two-year refurbishment. He's in the SDPD's holding cell at the moment."

Bull lit a Marlboro. "Well, the motive is obvious. Mary and Harvey meet, Mary gets a room and Harvey gets a surprise. A drunk Marine wanders into The Crying Game. Not the first time."

Starr had to agree. Even a hint of mint could sink a career in the Marines. Add booze to the panic?

"People have killed for less," he said.

"Okay, you've got to get on this case immediately," Bull told him. "What else do you have open at the moment?"

"Just the Pier 44 Bang-Bang thing," Starr replied.

Their office had received a tip two weeks ago that some rare combat-style weapons had been smuggled in via San Diego's Pier 44, virtually under the Navy's nose. The cache was said to contain sixty copies of a prototype rifle called the AR-8/9. It had been envisioned as a heavy assault weapon for the U.S. military back in the late 1950s. But the Pentagon eventually decided to go with the famous M-16.

Several dozen AR-8/9s were manufactured to be evaluated in a series of runoffs with the other competitors. When it lost, the manufacturer stuck the copies away in a warehouse. When the company went out of business, the guns were sold first to a museum in Mexico, then to a collector in Singapore. Somehow they wound up in the hands of what NILE was now calling the Pier 44 Gang.

But just who was in the gang and why they wanted the elderly weapons was still a mystery. The tipster said the AR-8/9s were going to be modified somehow, but into what—and whether any of this was even true—was also unclear.

"I'll take that case now," Bull said, crushing out his cigarette. "Text me the files. Meanwhile you go full time on the Dick Chick thing. DC will be on my ass, so I'm going to be on yours. Loop me with every move you make. And please, wrap it up quick, before the media sticks its nose in it."

Chapter Seven

"What's this going to cost me?"

The Navy secretary looked up at Starr. Her name was Holly. Very pretty. Very sexy. She was on the Admiral's staff; her office was four floors up from Starr's.

"Let me borrow your Jag for the weekend . . ." she replied.

Starr laughed. "Why do I have to bribe you at all? Isn't looking up stuff part of your job?"

"Yes, for *senior* officers," she said. "Not for the X-Files guys. Next you'll be asking me to type for you."

But she was already banging on her keyboard. The general performance file of the murder suspect, Captain Kyle Harvey, soon popped on her screen.

It was only a paragraph long; they read it together.

Harvey had no prior assaults on women or transgender people. No criminal transgressions, no reprimands at all.

"Your guy's a clean marine," Holly said. "Is he single?"

"What's in his service record?"

More banging on the keys.

"Two tours in Afghanistan as a weapons specialist," Holly reported. "One in Iraq with the SEALS as a master armorer."

"So, he's into guns," Starr mused. "Yet he chose to snap her neck."

*****

Harvey's quarters were on Sunset Drive, about a mile east of the Navy base. It was an apartment building leased for officers who had extended duty at the shipyard.

Starr picked the lock and went in clean. Building a hate crime case was difficult in any jurisdiction. Doing it for the military, with DC in their pants, meant zero margin for error. No loose ends, no fuck ups.

So Starr was praying he'd find a stack of white supremacist magazines, anti gender materials, a copy of *Mein Kampf*—anything to make this job easier. But besides needing a good dusting, Harvey's bachelor quarters were ship shape. Kitchen, living room, bedroom, bathroom. No fringe lit. No swastikas.

Starr turned on Harvey's computer and did a thorough sweep. No bondage, no porn of any kind. No visits to hate group sites and no evidence the hard drive had been scrubbed lately.

The attached one-car garage was also orderly if, again, dusty . . . except near a small corner workbench where a portable jeweler's lathe sat, a week-old repair ticket still attached. The floor below it had recently been swept.

Bull answered Starr's call on the first ring.

"The guy's a choir boy," Starr told him, giving him a quick report on what little he'd found. "He needs a cleaning lady, but that's about it. Do you want me to go back in and break down some walls? Look inside his mattress?"

"Don't bother," Bull told him. "Unless you think he's building a cross for the KKK, don't waste any more time there. Move on."

Chapter Eight

Starr's next stop was a dive bar in the Gaslight Quarter called Puffs. It was where Mary Contrary worked.

But he wanted to swing by home first.

Angel was just getting out of the shower when he came through the wormhole. Her hair up in a towel, her short bathrobe without a belt to keep it closed, she leaned out the bathroom door just enough for them to kiss, then went back to getting dressed. She smelled heavenly.

"Why are you damp?" she asked him.

"It's a long story," he called back to her, sitting on the edge of the bed. "Have you ever heard of a place called Puffs?"

"Nope . . . ."

"It's a tranny bar in the Gaslight Quarter."

"And you want to go there for dinner sometime?"

"It's the place of employment for the vic on the case I just caught."

She started drying her hair.

"How about you come with me?" he yelled over the blower. "You know, for support?"

He heard her laugh. "Sorry, honey, I've got a shoot at one o'clock. Besides, I'd be the only real girl there."

"Well, in theory . . ."

She walked out of the bathroom. "How do I look?"

Starr's jaw dropped. She was dressed as Supergirl. A very hot, sexy looking Supergirl. Top to bottom, boots to cape. Everything was blue and red, skintight and plunging.

"It's a superheroes theme for LA Vogue," she said, fluffing her hair. She struck a hands-on-hip pose. "Can you tell who I'm supposed to be?"

Starr could barely talk. This was just like a dream he'd had when he was eleven years old.

"Not Batman . . ." he finally blurted out.

"And you would be right," she said, grabbing her make-up bag for a final touch up.

Starr couldn't take his eyes off her. "When do you have to bring that back?"

"Open ended," she replied. "Why? Want me to get a Superman costume to go with it?"

Starr opened his mouth, but this time, nothing came out. She'd left him speechless. It happened a lot.

She walked over and kissed him deeply.

"Think about it," she said, wiping lipstick from his chin. "And if they have t-shirts at Puffs, will you get one for me?"

Chapter Nine

Puffs was packed.

Starr arrived at 12:05, five minutes after opening, hoping for an empty bar. He'd even tried to visualize the place with just the bartender there to talk to. But the vision didn't come true.

It wasn't a lunch-crowd crowd. It was a mourning party for Mary Contrary—and there was a definite theme. Five Lizas, five Chers. A couple Bette Midlers. A couple Marilyns. The subterranean room was a blur of long fingernails, giant eyelashes, vape smoke and perfume.

And Angel had been right. She would have been the only girl there.

The crowd parted when Starr appeared. He walked to the bar and pulled out Harvey's picture. He showed it to the bartender, who was channeling k.d. lang.

Had Harvey been in here before?

"He sure has," many voices replied at once.

The bartender nodded to a table at the back; the darkest spot in the place.

"His GI Joe friends dumped him there, blind drunk. They told him he was in a strip club and then left. Mary felt bad for him, sat with him. They wound up talking for hours—I took her shift."

A chorus of "Amens" went around the bar.

"Nothing was the same after that," k.d. added. "They were so lovey dovey. In fact, they were going to move in together."

The noise in Starr's head at that moment sounded just like a phonograph needle scratching a new vinyl record.

He had to interrupt. "All that happened *last* night?'

k.d. shook her head. "No, honey—it was three months ago. That guy practically lived here after that. He and Mary were exclusive."

Chapter Ten

Starr stepped out onto the street, Puffs t-shirt in hand. His phone buzzed. It was Bull.

"Tell me everything, Lieutenant . . ."

"Our clean marine was no stranger to Puffs," Starr reported. "He's been a regular there for months."

"You sure he just didn't need stronger glasses?"

"The boys say he and Mary were picking out china patterns."

Bull snorted. "What the fuck are they teaching these guys at Parris Island?"

"It might change everything," Starr told him. "Was this a hate crime—stemming from a huge misunderstanding? Or was it really a lovers' spat?"

"Bullshit on that," Bull huffed back. "DC isn't going to buy a love story between a Marine captain and a tranny. So get some hate evidence fast—make it up if you have to."

Bull hung up—but Starr's phone immediately buzzed again.

It was Angel.

"I'm on my way to the superheroes shoot, but your machine picked up a message for you just as I was leaving. It was Sergeant Falconi down at the lockup; he tried your cell phone but couldn't get it to ring. You really need a new phone, love. I think enough time has passed since . . ."

He gently interrupted her; "And the message was?"

"Let's see—your latest collar, Captain Harvey, is telling people down at the jail that he'll plead guilty and take whatever punishment comes with it. Sergeant Falconi suggests you get down there quick."

Chapter Eleven

Starr was at the lock up in minutes. In pure speed, the mad dash from the Gaslight District rivaled his car chase earlier in the day.

He was let into Harvey's holding cell and closed the door behind him.

Rock-jawed and chiseled, Harvey was a living example of why all white guys who shave their heads resemble serial killers. He was a scary-looking dude.

Yet he was in the corner of the cell, still on the bunk, leaning against the wall in a vertical fetal position, clearly in distress. He could barely look at Starr

"Remember me?" Starr asked him.

"How could I forget?" Harvey replied, rubbing his swollen jaw.

"You're doing a stupid thing, Captain. Right or wrong, copping a guilty plea is foolish. You know how screwed up military justice is."

Harvey just looked away. "I know you want to charge me with a hate crime—but I don't care. I killed Mary in a fit of rage, OK? She tricked me and I was ashamed by what my brother Marines would think of me. Happy?"

"But why BS me?" Starr asked him. "I know there's more to it. More to you and Mary."

Harvey's face turned dark crimson.

"I don't care what you know, lieutenant," he spit back at Starr. "That's the statement. No lawyers. No court martial. Felony hate crime and murder? No problem. I just need to get this over with."

Starr didn't know what else to say to the guy, so he left and called Bull immediately. The boss was hugely relieved on hearing his report.

"Now we can give DC exactly what it wants wrapped in a bow," he told Starr in a tone that for Bull sounded close to joy. "Case closed."

Chapter Twelve

"Nothing feels right . . ."

"Are you saying you don't want to marry me?"

Starr rolled his eyes. He couldn't help it. He was lying on the bed with Angel, TV on, but muted. She was reading, glasses on, looking sexy. But he was distracted and watching the lights from outside make strange shadows on the ceiling.

"A million guys would want to marry you," he told her. "Tens of millions. I'm just the lucky one."

And he meant it. He loved her so much that if this wasn't the real thing, then he had a serious mental problem.

"Then why did you say that?" she wanted to know.

"Just thinking about today's collar," he said. "The Dick Chick thing."

"'The Dick Chick thing?' That's offensive."

"I know. It's just easier to say."

She closed her book and took off her glasses. "What doesn't feel right about a Marine jock who murdered his transvestite girlfriend? It's got Netflix Original written all over it."

"But I know he didn't kill Mary in some kind of sudden panic about being discovered with her. He loved her.

It *wasn't* a hate crime. So why doesn't he care if we charge him with one?"

Angel snuggled up to him. "Maybe it's more embarrassing that he actually had long-term feelings for her. Think of the soap opera that court martial would be."

"Maybe . . ." Starr sighed. "Or—he's covering up something else."

"Something more unusual than a transvestite love affair?"

He finally kissed her. "Anything's possible, doll face . . ."

Chapter Thirteen

The next morning. 0600 hours.

Starr pulled the Jag up to the security gate leading into the Navy's shipyard repair docks; Harvey's ship was undergoing its refit here.

His NILE badge got him by the guards. He found the USS *Stone* about a hundred yards down the pier.

Even in a state of repair, it was an impressive ship. Guided missile cruisers were the beasts of the Navy. Deck guns, Gatling guns. Cruise missiles, anti-ship missiles, anti-aircraft missiles. Fifty cals everywhere. Awesomeness atop water.

He needed to see the ship's personnel records—or at least that's what he told the officer of the deck once he got past the two marines stationed at the gangway. Truth was, Dick Chick wasn't Starr's case anymore. Bull had typed up the 26-page charge form himself—strange as until now, the NILE West office just assumed the boss couldn't type. He'd also filled in all the evidence sheets, attached all the crime scene photos and forensics reports and then copied everything in quadruplicate—by himself. Without anyone else reading it, Bull sent the entire hate crime dossier to Washington sometime before midnight.

As a result, Starr knew he'd be back on the Pier 44 Bang-Bang case as soon as he walked into his office.

But he had to see one more thing first.

The officer of the deck heard him out. It was no secret that Harvey was in jail for murder. The victim's identity had yet to be revealed, but it was only a matter of time before it leaked out. Starr was straightforward with his request, but gave no details.

Inside of five minutes, he was in a private cabin, scrolling through Harvey's on-board personnel file.

Sexual proclivities aside, the clean marine just seemed too clean to him. He'd been on the USS *Stone* for 15 months. Had he been a choir boy at sea too?

It seemed so—at first.

But after scanning a multitude of documents, Starr came upon a tiny addendum to something called the Watch Commander's Report.

It showed Harvey had a single blemish. He'd been stopped at the Navy Base's main gate two weeks before with portable lathe he'd taken from the ship without permission. His punishment: one day's duty in the ship's laundry.

Starr was back in the Jag minutes later.

The guards at the front gate saluted and waved him through. But he still wasn't going to the office—not just yet.

Chapter Fourteen

Ten minutes later, he was back inside Harvey's apartment.

In Starr's semi beautiful mind, the question wasn't so much why Harvey might need a lathe so badly that he stole one while his own was being repaired. It was, why sweep the garage floor and not your own kitchen?

Starr went right to the garage, this time armed with a flashlight. He studied the spot under the work bench that had been swept and then trained the light on the wall behind it. A reflection caught his eye, something shimmering like a diamond.

He pulled out a piece of metal about four inches long with the circumference of his middle finger. One end had been recently machined and then filed down to what looked like exacting proportions. It had been polished and that's why it was shining.

Starr immediately knew what he was looking at: a firing bolt for a combat assault rifle.

The Bang-Bang Case. The shipment of old AR-8/9s rifles. Someone turning them into . . . what?

Starr hadn't been sure until that moment.

But now he knew.

The AR-8/9 was not much different in design from the ubiquitous Russian made Kalashnikov AK-47 assault rifle; in fact, its creators' intention was to build an American version of the powerful AK.

With a few modifications and a few parts copped from the infamous Kalashnikov, it would be easy to transform an AR-8/9 into a sort of cheaply made super gun very similar to the AK-47. High rate of fire, full auto, thirty rounds a clip. That's a bad news shooter, especially if you're facing one.

But because the AR-8/9 was designed to fire a slightly smaller round than the Kalashnikov, any AK firing bolt would have to be machined down to be slightly smaller and shorter as well.

And that's exactly what Starr was holding in his hand.

Chapter Fifteen

Starr finally made it to the office by 0800.

Bull was already there. He was sitting at his desk, dunking a doughnut into his tea. But he froze as soon as Starr walked in. He knew the junior officer's expression well.

"Oh, Christ. I have one fucking doughnut a year and now I can't enjoy it, can I?"

"I've got a new theory on the Dick Chick case," Starr said, sitting down across from him.

Bull's face darkened. "But you're not on that case anymore. Neither am I. It's in DC, it's their baby now."

"Well, it might get bounced back to us. I just found evidence that Harvey could be involved in the Pier 44 case."

Bull was so startled he dropped the entire doughnut into his cup.

Starr showed him the machined firing bolt.

"He stole a portable lathe from his ship when his own was broken, that's how important it was to him. And he did precision work. The question is, why would this guy be so diligently cutting firing bolts in his garage?"

"Wasn't he an armorer or something for the SEALs?"

"And so, he misses fixing guns?"

Bull put his head in his hands—and stayed like that for more than a minute.

"You know, I have two huge alimony payments due tomorrow," he moaned. "And I could barely afford that doughnut. Just once, I'd like everything to go smoothly."

He finally sat up and wiped his eyes.

"OK, you're back on the case," he told Starr. "Go talk to Harvey, and this time, take the time to get the what's what."

Chapter Sixteen

Harvey looked even more distraught than the last time Starr had seen him.

Ashen, unshaven, sweating profusely. He was still cuffed to the bunk, still in a fetal position against the wall.

Again, Starr closed the door behind him, leaving the marine guard to go get a coffee.

"How much does it cost to have a jewelers' lathe repaired these days, Captain Harvey?" he asked him.

The marine hardly moved. "How would I know?" he replied, his voice raspy and just above a whisper.

"Well, you just had yours fixed. I saw the receipt. Did the bit assembly wear out? Must have been something major for you to risk a day in the ship's laundry to use one of Uncle Sam's."

"I don't know what you're talking about, lieutenant . . ."

Starr threw the cut firing bolt onto the bunk.

"Why waste time here, Captain? I know why you've been machining those firing bolts. That's old news. The latest is our forensics lab knows exactly how many bolts you cut and they have proof of what they were going to be used for."

This was a lie. NILE didn't have a forensics lab. They sent everything to Quantico—and it took forever to get anything back.

But Harvey bought it. He deflated even further.

"The 'Kalashnikov Kiss," he moaned. "That's what they call the modification. But God damn I wish I'd never heard those words."

Starr pulled a chair close to the bunk.

"Look, I'm probably the only other person in this world who's not a transvestite that knows this isn't just about Mary. You *loved* Mary. This is about those firing bolts, too, and where they went."

Harvey finally broke. He began sobbing. "I did love her. As fucked up as that sounds. I never saw it coming; it was like I was in another world. But when some of these wise guys found out and knew I'd been an armorer for the SEALs, they blackmailed me. I couldn't get out."

"But why kill her?"

"I *had* to. She walked in on us one night when they were picking up the cut bolts. I begged them to keep her out of it, but she saw them and what we were doing, so she had to go. They told me to do her, or they would— and then they'd kill me too. So I did it as quick as possible . . . so she wouldn't suffer."

"You said: 'wise guys?'" Starr asked him. "You mean the Mob is behind this? Running assault rifles? That doesn't sound like them."

Harvey laughed through his tears. "I wish it was the Mob. The Mob I could handle. No, it's these wacko gun-runners, the ones who smuggled in those old guns in the first place. They're all hardened combat vets and they're all from some 'hood, somewhere. And that's what they're going to do with these 'Super-89s' they call them. They're going to sell them in the barrios up in LA."

Starr had to stop him there. "You're saying a bunch of veterans smuggled those guns in?"

"Ex-*special forces* veterans," Harvey explained wearily. "Black ops guys. Real actors. They're all fucked up on painkillers and opioids and they need help. But the Veterans Administration just kept screwing them over. Their benefits sucked to the point that they just said Fuck It, got together and started making money doing something they know how to do. But, let me repeat, they're *psychos*. They think they're inside their own real life video game. They love the violence. They love big toys and loud noises. And once they find out that I'm here, and that I've ratted them out, they'll want to whack me too."

Now it made sense to Starr. "And that's why you wanted to plead out? To get somewhere safer than this lock up?"

Harvey put his head against the wall. "Yes—but I know it's just putting off the inevitable. These guys can find anyone anywhere. They're pros. And when you're in their sights, they never miss."

"That's unlikely," Starr told him matter of factly. "But I'll promise you this: while I'm on this job I'll protect you with my life."

No sooner were the words out of his mouth when the cell's window exploded in a storm of broken glass and high caliber gunfire. Starr pushed Harvey to the floor, painfully stretching the handcuffs but saving his life. The barrage perforated the wall in front of them.

The second burst was longer, louder and much closer to where they were lying, flat on the floor. It took out what was left of the wall. In seconds, the holding cell was more than half destroyed.

Harvey yelled over the roar: "*See what I mean?*"

Chapter Seventeen

Starr's higher instincts had just one suggestion: *Move quickly.*

He unlocked the handcuff holding Harvey to the bunk, attached it to the marine's other wrist and then dragged him across the floor towards the door. A third barrage came through the window, the most intense yet. It decimated what remained of the wall and broke through to the hallway beyond.

Starr and Harvey were covered with white dust by the time they got out of the cell. Luckily the hallway was empty. Crouched low, boots clanging on the metal stairs, Starr led Harvey down to the station's back door, at the same time managing to call Bull.

The boss picked up on the first ring.

"Short version, sir. I'm at the lockup. I've confirmed Harvey is part of the Pier 44 Gang. Mary stumbled onto them and they ordered him to kill her."

"So . . . please tell me: *now* is the case closed?"

"Not exactly," Starr replied. "We have an unanticipated problem. The Pier 44 guys have found Harvey and they're currently shooting fifty cals at us. So, we are egressing the lockup."

Starr heard Bull yell: "Jesus Christ! Okay, stay cool . . . I'll track you and send help, but make sure you don't . . ."

But suddenly Bull wasn't there. Starr's dumb phone had died. He started banging it on his knee, then turning it off and right back on again. But it was hopeless. It wouldn't come back to life.

They went out the station's rear door as dozens of SD police were rushing to the jail cells, responding to the sounds of gunfire. The last thing Starr wanted was to get them involved. This was still a military matter.

So he threw Harvey into the Jag, attached the hand-cuffs to the seat brace and took off.

But to where?

Chapter Eighteen

Starr's pre-cog was buzzing, telling him to get back to the base.

His job now was to keep Harvey alive. But if their would-be killers had the nuts to shoot up a police station with combat weapons, then no place in the civilian world would be safe. At least at the base he could find help and get shelter.

He screeched onto Sea Street and headed south at high speed. Night had fallen. The moon was up. And, oddly, traffic was nonexistent.

Starr's phone suddenly rang, working again.

It was Bull.

"Where are you?"

"At Sea and Exchange Streets, just going through the light now."

"OK—play it cool. I'm on this."

But then the phone went dead again

Starr roared through the next intersection; still no traffic. On a Friday night? Why wasn't anyone on Exchange Street?

Suddenly, he saw a quick vision of the very near future.

"Oh fuck . . ."

He pushed Harvey to the floor and steered hard left. The screech was louder than Starr could have imagined. An all black Hummer appeared in front of them a moment later.

It had come out of an alley to his right. At least four people inside were shooting at him, including the driver. And they were close enough for Starr to see their weapons: AR-8/9s . . . with the Kalashnikov Kiss.

He swerved into the Hummer—the driver instinctively turned away. Starr then put the Jag into a 180 while retrieving his Glock from his side holster.

The Hummer was starting to turn back towards him; Starr went hard left and aimed right for them. But then he went hard right, crossing the T as the old Navy bucks would say. He began firing directly out his window at the men in the Hummer while they were in a position where they couldn't really get a clear shot at him.

Starr put five rounds into the windshield and the driver's side door. The barrage barely bruised the Hummer. The steel was reinforced, the glass was bulletproof. No surprise. But it did hinder the driver's view.

Starr swerved left again, winding up on the Hummer's tail. As it tried to turn into him, he put a couple more rounds into the rear window. Again, the glass reacted like it had been hit by a couple powder bombs. But now the driver's rear view was obscured as well.

Starr went right again so sharply, the Jag's wheels left the pavement. He was intent on lining up another shot at the windshield; a couple lucky hits in the same place might break on through. But just as he was putting another clip in his Glock, a long streak of red fire went over their heads and exploded in the shallow bay across from Front Street.

Harvey yelped when it went over. Incredibly, someone had just fired an RPG at them. Starr thought out loud: "OK, now it's serious . . ."

Busting caps was one thing. Going up against rocket propelled grenades was another. Time for a graceful exit.

Starr stood on the accelerator and the Jag's dozen cylinders responded. The car took off like a rocket, leaving their attackers far behind.

He drove the length of Front Street at 100 mph, and then squealed back onto Harborside. He was now just a mile from the base's main gate.

Then his phone came alive again.

It was Bull. "What's your location, lieutenant?"

"On Harborside, heading south. We're just leaving an exchange of heavy ordinance at the corner of Exchange and Seaside. It was the same guys who shot up central booking. Multiple assault rifles and at least one

RPG fired at us. I'm presently heading for the base at flank speed. ETA, three minutes."

There was a fierce burst of static, then Bull came back on.

"That's a negative on returning to the base," he told Starr. "They have no idea you're coming or what might be following you. Too many non-combatants around for that. Divert to the L-Wing on Standard Ave instead. Do you remember where that is?"

Starr immediately felt uneasy. The L-Wing was an abandoned mental institution about a half mile this side of the base. The San Diego cops sometimes took hostage rescue training there. A rambling, imposing building from the late 30s, the uneven blotches on its faded red bricks always reminded Starr of dried blood.

And that wasn't the only thing about the L-Wing that gave him the creeps.

Chapter Nineteen

Starr fishtailed onto Bay Street and then drove up Standard Ave to what the locals called Bishop's Heights.

Here was the long shuttered San Diego L-Wing Mental Institution. Ancient black gates, long crumbling driveway, the building with the bloody bricks sat on a rise, dark and foreboding. Overgrown weeping willows surrounded it, wrapping the place in gloom.

Starr crept up the driveway, headlights doused, rolling to a stop in front of the old hospital's main entrance. He scanned the vicinity. No other vehicles parked nearby, no lights on inside the building itself. Still, a familiar apprehension was building in his chest.

He parked in the shadows and shut down the engine. Harvey was still crunched on the floor; he hadn't moved since the gun battle. If this were a movie, the Marine would have been killed by a stray bullet during the shootout—but no. Starr had driven so aggressively during the ambush nothing had hit them.

He jostled Harvey back to life. "We're taking a walk . . ."

Starr unlocked the handcuffs from the seat brace, pulled Harvey out the driver's side door and re-cuffed him. He grabbed two extra ammo clips, but couldn't find his penlight. He took a Bic lighter instead. They made their way up the steps and into the long shuttered infirmary.

The darkened main lobby was all cold marble and peeling paint. By the faint glow of the Bic, it looked right out of a 1930s horror movie.

Starr's phone rang, making both of them jump. It was Bull.

"Where are you, lieutenant?"

"L-Wing—main lobby. As ordered . . ."

"OK, roger that. Stay in place. We're on the way."

Starr sat Harvey down in front of the timeworn admitting desk and then slid down next to him.

He turned the lighter off, plunging them into darkness.

This was not a happy place for Starr.

Pre-cog shrinkage had some very weird side effects. He went to his first funeral at the age of 8. It was for an uncle he'd never met and just six people were in attendance. Yet as soon as he stepped into the church, his head was flooded with voices, hundreds of conversations going on at once. Men, women, kids. He was nauseous for the entire service and it didn't go away until he left the church.

He'd never mentioned this to anyone—except the Navy shrinks and that was a big mistake. They grilled him about it and other similar occurrences he'd had as a kid. Their over-the-top curiosity both concerned and baffled him. They obviously thought there was some connection to his pre-cog ability, but they didn't know what. After interviewing him for hours, one doctor wrote in his personnel file "subject sometimes feels the presence of the deceased." Another wrote: "If subject ever actually sees any phantasm, he must report it to us immediately."

Now Starr's forehead began to hurt. The chorus of the deceased he'd heard in the church that day, and a few times since, he was hearing again right now in spades, a very unpleasant feeling. This was a definite downside to his abilities. It didn't happen very often, but when it did, he would have traded it for vertigo, agoraphobia, fear of flying—*anything* was better than this.

Five minutes passed; each one more uncomfortable than the last. He tried blocking his ears, but that didn't work. He tried to distract himself by calling Bull back, but his phone refused to work. He simply tried to ignore the ethereal chorus, but that was impossible. He even asked Harvey if he was hearing anything unusual.

The marine responded in the negative, but added, "I've played with guns most of my adult life, so I'm down to thirty-percent hearing."

Five more minutes went by, excruciating for Starr as now the voices had transformed in wails and he felt he could hear the cries of every poor soul who'd passed away inside this miserable place.

But then, suddenly, he heard something else: Car doors slamming. Footsteps, running. And *real* voices, calling out to one another. Starr sat up just in time to see three ghostly figures pass by the hospital's broken front windows.

"Please tell me your boss is finally here," Harvey said, watching it all too.

But Starr stayed frozen to the spot, still uneasy. Was this Bull's rescue team? Or someone else?

His question was answered an instant later when the building's front doors blew open in a massive explosion. The barrage of gunfire that followed rivaled the ones back at central booking.

They both hit the floor and covered their heads.

Amidst the chaos and noise, Harvey yelled over to Starr: "I just *knew* it wouldn't be this easy . . ."

Chapter Twenty

Suddenly Starr's phone rang. It was Bull.

He fought to hear his boss over the roar of heavy caliber machine guns.

"Where *the hell* are you?" Bull yelled at him.

"Same location last time you called," Starr yelled back. "But we're not the only ones here. A bunch of vehicles just arrived outside and now we're taking heavy fire again. I'm guessing this isn't your rescue force?"

"No," Bull replied. "Our guys are in the air, but still a few minutes out."

Starr asked: "Any suggestions?"

"You need a really good place to hide," Bull replied. "I just got an ATF schematic of that place. North corner, subbasement, there's a room made of concrete one foot thick. It's where they stuck troublesome patients as punishment. There's a red light bulb above the doorframe. Get there quick, lock yourselves in and don't move until we arrive. Repeat: stay in position so we know where to find you."

Then the phone went dead again.

Keeping low under the nonstop fusillade, Starr and Harvey zig-zagged out of the lobby and into a stairwell. Starr didn't dare light the Bic, so they went down three floors in complete darkness, tripping over the debris left from decades of decay. With each step Starr tried to concentrate only on real sounds, not ghostly ones. But the deeper they went inside the old sanatorium, the more raucous the unearthly cries became.

They reached the subbasement and started towards the north end of the building, the glow of the Bic at last lighting their way. Trudging along the winding corridor, it sounded like dozens of footsteps were following right behind them. Starr turned a couple times to look, only to see nothing but the grim darkness.

Just as the Bic was starting to fail, they found the door with the red bulb above it. Shutting off the lighter to preserve fluid, they were plunged into complete darkness again. It took a few tries, but Starr finally pushed the heavy door open. They went inside and closed it behind them.

Starr lit the Bic again, just for a few seconds to look for the door's lock. He couldn't find it on the first sweep, but he did see that the room was indeed made of thick concrete—the walls, ceiling and floor appeared slathered in it. But he could also see scratches all over the walls, as if hundreds of fingernails had tried to tear their way through the concrete. He could understand why some poor souls who got locked in here would want to get out.

But what drove them to try to claw their way through the walls with their bare hands?

Starr's unease rocketed. He doused the Bic and, while Harvey continued the search for the door's lock in the complete darkness, he began banging on his phone again, hoping to bring it back to life.

Incredibly, it started buzzing.

It was Bull, of course—and he always had the same question.

"Where are you, lieutenant?"

"In the rubber room in the L-Wing's subbasement" Starr replied. "As instructed. Trying to find a way to lock the door."

"OK—just hang on. We're getting close."

But Starr needed more than that. "Do you have an ETA? Are you coming in force, I hope?"

"We're about a minute away," his boss replied, sounding peeved. "Don't move again until we get there. Are you listening? *Remain in place . . .*"

But Starr had already closed his flip phone.

Something was very wrong here. If this was a room where they put problem patients, would there really be a lock on the inside of the door?

Then, suddenly . . . on the wall outside, a loud scratching. Like someone was scraping the old concrete.

Starr tensed. Was this really happening? But then he felt Harvey's hand squeeze him on the shoulder. He heard it too.

"Someone's putting explosives on the outside wall," the marine whispered urgently. "They're scraping the surface so the charges' adhesive will stick better."

"Jessuzz," Starr breathed. "Now it's plastic explosives?" The scraping got louder.

"You're the expert," he said to Harvey. "What's the fuse time on something like this?"

Harvey thought a moment. "Enclosed area, below the foundation line? Once they've activated the charges, maybe a half minute tops. Just enough time for them to get to cover."

Starr checked his Glock. He had six rounds in the clip, and two clips in his pockets. He reached down to his ankle holster and pulled out his back-up weapon: a 357 Magnum, fully loaded.

He unlocked Harvey's handcuffs and then handed him the giant pistol.

The marine was shocked. He tried to push the gun back into Starr's hands.

"You're kidding right? Yesterday, you were chasing me like a madman and you couldn't wait to get me in cuffs. Now you're giving me this?"

"Those are the bad guys out there," Starr told him grimly, feeling his life suddenly ticking away. "And the cavalry probably won't arrive in time. We both know how this movie's going to end. What else can we do but go out shooting?"

Suddenly the scraping noise stopped. The explosives were in place.

But then, another sound, unmistakable and done seemingly as an afterthought. It was that of a bolt being slid into place—on the outside of the door. Starr tried the door and found it impossible to budge.

His fear from a moment ago had come true. This room was basically a jail cell. Of course, the lock was on the outside.

This reality was chilling and unexpected. Even shooting their way out was no longer an option.

They were trapped.

"We got about twenty seconds before those charges blow." Harvey told him. "What do we do now?"

Chapter Twenty-One

The Pier 44 Gang was organized along military lines.

Captains and soldiers. Squads and small platoons. They even had their own sapper team, six men, all schooled in the art of combat explosives. They were called on when the gang needed something—or someone—blown up.

They were here in the subbasement of the L-Wing, taking cover in an old employees' cafeteria. Along with a couple dozen of their colleagues scattered throughout the building, these men were in pursuit of Captain Kyle Harvey with orders to terminate him.

They knew their target was not alone. Two men had been inside the SDPD jail cell when the gang shot it up. Because they'd escaped together, the gang assumed the second guy was Harvey's attorney, though after the gun battle on Exchange Street, it was hard to believe any lawyer could drive or shoot like that.

In any case, they'd cornered the pair in the building's old rubber room and had wired it to blow.

And blow it did.

The explosion shook the old building top to bottom. After waiting for the dust to settle, three of the sappers went back down the hallway to check the damage and confirm the fatalities. A pool among the gang had a $5,000 bonus going to the first team to take down the prey. The sappers were sure they had that money in their pockets.

But suddenly came the sound of gunfire from the direction of the explosion, intense but brief.

Then, silence.

Mystified, the remaining gunmen went to investigate. They made their way down the corridor, to the rubber room—or what was left of it.

Their explosives had done their work almost too well. The rubber room no longer existed. It had been devastated along with a lot of the hallway. And there were two dead bodies lying atop the rubble.

But the deceased were not Harvey and his gunslinger lawyer. Rather they were two of their sapper comrades. Both had been shot in the head.

The third man was lying atop the rubble as well; he had a massive wound in his leg. They dragged him back to the lunch room, propped him up against a table, tied off the wound and injected him with four clips of morphine.

Only then did they ask him what happened.

"Those bastards came right at us, right out of the smoke," the man reported shakily. "Firing hand cannons."

He looked down at his wound. It looked like bloody chopped beef.

"Oh, Christ . . ." he whispered.

But why weren't their two would be victims killed in the blast? How did they get out?

The wounded man jammed two more morphine sticks into his upper thigh, but they didn't do much good. He was going into shock.

"I got no fucking idea," he said, losing consciousness. "Maybe they're superheroes . . ."

Starr was wondering something like that himself.

Whenever a flash of pre-cog hit him, it was always best to follow it. As the seconds had ticked down inside the rubber room, locked in and about to be blown to bits, his instincts told him he and Harvey should squeeze into the room's northwest corner, just behind the door. There was no time to question it. He threw Harvey in that direction just as the explosives went off.

The blast was tremendous. The smoke was suffocating and the walls around them turned to dust. But when they could see again, astonished to be alive, they discovered they were standing underneath a series of steel beams with a network of old pipes running through them. The pipes and the beams had been plastered-over years before to blend in with the concrete, only to be exposed by the explosion.

The room had collapsed on itself, but the steel ceiling had prevented the huge chunks of falling concrete from crushing them to death, while the thick door had shielded them from the flames. And it was the only place in the room that had this unexpected protection. A half foot either way and they would have been toast.

But why was this steel ceiling here?

Starr saw the old pipes were perforated with uniformly placed half-inch holes, almost like an antique sprinkler system. He reached up, ran his hand along a few of the holes, then took a sniff. His fingers smelled like almonds.

Cyanide . . .

There was only one explanation. Patients deemed too difficult for the staff to deal with, must have been locked in this room and quietly gassed to death . . . in the 1930s. That's why the walls were covered with fingernail scratches.

No wonder Starr had been hearing voices.

The place was haunted . . .

He and Harvey were waiting when the first three gang members came to inspect their handiwork. The trio of sappers were caught off-guard, it was a quick, one-sided gunfight. Starr wounded the man in the leg; Harvey killed the other two.

But now they were running and the marine was close to going into shock himself. Stumbling through the dark hallways, heading even deeper into the bowels of the hospital trying to escape, Harvey's dazed state had little to do with the two men he'd just shot to death.

He simply couldn't believe he was still alive.

He kept muttering the same thing between gasping breaths. "How did that happen? How *the fuck* did that just happen?"

But Starr was worried about more immediate things.

While he kept pushing Harvey to move faster, even though they were running blind, he had no idea where they were going.

In cases like this, it was always wise to seek higher ground. But since the explosion had gone off, it sounded like a hundred gang members were running through the halls, all of them in hot pursuit. And Starr knew these sounds were for real.

He also knew that despite Bull's orders, it was time to get out of the L-Wing.

But how? He wasn't even sure where they were in relation to the outside. They didn't want to fall into the waiting arms of the gunmen.

Suddenly his phone rang.

It was Bull—and he was furious.

"Where *the fuck* are you, lieutenant?" he bellowed.

"Someone wired up the rubber room," Starr told him between deep gasps. "We had to move or we would have been blown up."

"Listen to me Lieutenant Starr," Bull told him. "We're less than two minutes away. Do not . . ."

But before he could finish the sentence, Starr's phone went dead again.

It didn't matter. Starr already knew what he was going to do.

Next right . . .

He pushed Harvey into the next room they came to. It was a storage locker, with a thick window that had been painted over to keep the sun out—and no door. It looked to Starr that he'd have to break through the thick window to get out. The problem was, he wasn't sure he could do it.

So Harvey did it for him.

The marine put his head down and ran into the glass like he was splitting a couple linebackers. There was a great crash, and Harvey tumbled into the parking lot. Starr fell out right after him.

Only when he was able to reorient himself did Starr realize his instinct had been right on again.

They'd burst out of the building not ten feet from where he'd parked the Jag.

Chapter Twenty-Two

They were roaring down the driveway of the L-Wing not twenty seconds later.

But where to go *now*?

The Navy Base was still out. Bull was already royally pissed at Starr for not staying put—twice—inside the L-Wing. He couldn't imagine the wrath he'd incur if he went back to base and a shootout resulted in casualties. Just about everyone in law enforcement would agree: Innocents always seemed to get hurt in gun battles that could have been avoided.

He needed to hide, for twenty minutes tops, just long enough for the rescue force to catch up. Someplace close, someplace dark but recognizable. A place their saviors would not have to waste time looking for.

Somewhere they could actually stay in place, until Bull's cavalry arrived.

Midway . . .

Starr took a quick left on Rosewood and got the Jag back up to 100 MPH. Tearing south for six blocks, he hit the brakes and took a violent right hand turn onto the waterfront. This was Coronado Wharf, the location of the USS *Midway* floating museum.

The highly decorated aircraft carrier had been retired in the 90s, and was now permanently docked as a showpiece for the Navy. The tourists loved it, but by luck it was closed for the night.

Starr screeched to a halt next to the old carrier. It was a real monster up close. One thousand feet long, 160-wide, with a big flat top full of old aircraft. It would be impossible for the rescue team to miss.

He checked his six, three and twelve. All was clear. His was the only car on the wharf. He pulled the Jag behind a visitor's tent, parking it deep in the shadow of the giant warship, hoping it would be safe.

A gangway used for tourist groups was still deployed. Starr busted the weak chain, letting him and Harvey in. They hurried up the walkway, through an open hatch and found themselves in the carrier's gift shop, mid-ship, 3-Level, meaning three below the flight deck.

Starr's phone rang. It was Bull, always right on cue.

"Where *the hell* are you, lieutenant?" he asked almost wearily.

Starr gave him their exact location, then began a brief description of their perilous escape from the L-Wing.

But Bull didn't care.

"This is a direct order," he seethed at Starr, temper in full fury. "Stay in that fucking gift shop. I repeat, *stay in place.* We are on the way."

But Starr had to get one question in. "Is this still a copter extraction?"

Bull roared back at him: "Of course it is, lieutenant!"

"Then, shouldn't we be up on the . . ."

But Bull had already hung up. Starr unflipped his phone. ". . . the flight deck?"

He looked at Harvey, who only shrugged. "That would seem to be the thing to do."

Suddenly the quiet of the waterfront was broken. Tires squealing, two black Escalades roared up to the gangway. Armed men in special forces gear started piling out of them.

Any chance *this* was Bull's rescue party went up in smoke when a third vehicle arrived also traveling at high speed. It was a black Hummer and it was peppered with bullet holes. The same monster they'd fought on Exchange Street.

In seconds, an army of two dozen gunmen had assembled on the dock. Each was carrying a Super-89 assault rifle, courtesy of the Kalashnikov Kiss.

Starr took it all in gloomily. Whether they'd been followed from the L-Wing or this was an entirely different unit of the Pier 44 Gang, clearly these people were out for blood.

That Starr hesitated even a moment was testament to his respect, aka fear, of Bull Parades. The most important aspect of any rescue mission was that those being rescued had to do everything they could to stay in one place. Let the rescuers come to you. Starr had violated that cardinal rule more than once tonight. And with each phone call from the boss, with each hangup and each time Starr's phone simply went dead, he could feel Bull's steam pressure rise.

But just like the other times, they had no choice but to move again.

The armed men on the dock set up a ragged firing line and, on a voice command, launched a furious barrage into the museum's gift shop.

It was violent and noisy—that was the point. These men were hunters. Their prey was inside the ship. The earsplitting fusillade was all about forcing the victims deeper inside the boat. Then, with superior numbers and firepower, the gang could corner them in a kill zone and finally put an end to this.

But as it turned out, the bombastic barrage wasn't necessary. Starr and Harvey had started running deeper into the ship long before the first spray of bullets hit the gift shop.

Chapter Twenty-Three

The Pier 44 gang members flooded onto the aircraft carrier and split into four groups, three Hammer squads plus the Anvil team.

The Hammer squads fanned out on the first three decks of the huge ship, making their presence known by banging on pipes and firing off random bursts from their Super-89s. Meanwhile the Anvil team quietly moved along their flank. Human nature said the prey will move away from the racket—and right into the guns of these noiseless troops. The Pier 44 gang knew this tactic well.

But Starr and Harvey knew what the gang was up to and, as a headgame, Hammer & Anvil could be an effective strategy. But take away the candy coating and it was still a grid-pattern search. The challenge was to go against one's basic instincts and not move away from the frightening sounds coming towards you.

When they turn one way—up, down, left, right—always turn with them and keep your courage up. If everybody keeps turning at right angles, which was rule one in the canon of grid searches, eventually you'll find a way to escape . . . or you'll run into the Anvil soldiers. But most likely you'll come up in back of them.

But the Pier 44 Gang weren't amateurs; they'd added their own twist to the strategy: the Anvil guys left booby traps in their wake, like human mouse traps, protecting their rear.

Starr and Harvey became painfully aware of this when they reached a stairwell that led directly to the carrier's flight deck, Starr's ultimate goal. Escape to the top, be visible for the rescue team and, when it was over, hope for the best the next time he saw Bull.

They'd managed to avoid all of the gang members' sweeps and now here was a ladder to the stars. They could hear one of the Hammer teams making a racket one passageway over and they'd just made a pivot away from them. So Starr and Harvey began quietly climbing the stairs.

That's when the bomb went off.

It was an ISB—an Israeli Smoke Bomb. About a half pound of explosive, some of it *plastique,* but most of it potassium chlorate mixed with sugar. The result: a blinding flash and lots of smoke. ISBs didn't kill; they made their victims disoriented and thus easier targets to be eliminated. Ghoulish in a way, but it was another favorite of Special Forces groups everywhere.

Starr wasn't looking directly into the flash when the ISB exploded, so his eyes were spared. But he got a lungful of smoke; it was sickly sweet and so thick he could barely see his hands in front of him.

Then the gunfire erupted. The flashes looked like lightning in a storm. Starr hit the deck, certain they'd walked into an ambush and that the gang members were mowing them down.

But that was not so. Harvey was doing all the shooting. Standing straight up, in a two handed combat stance, he pulled the Magnum's trigger four times in quick succession. When the smoke finally cleared, Starr saw four bodies sprawled on the stairs just above them.

They had come up in back of the Anvil team as predicted, setting off a bomb the gang had just left behind. But it all happened so quickly, the four gunmen were dead before they knew what hit them.

When it was over, Harvey stared at the pistol in disbelief.

"I was working with these guys just a few days ago," he said, now looking down at the bodies. "And like those two guys back at the nuthouse, I didn't even know their names."

Starr grabbed two Super-89s, four banana clips and gave Harvey a push. They started running now, up the stairs towards the flight deck.

And *that's* when they came face to face with four of the Hammer soldiers.

Starr and Harvey had reached the 2-deck, one down from the flat top, when a hatch right in front of them began to twist open. It swung towards them, so Starr and Harvey fired blindly into the opening. One man fell dead instantly; totally surprised, the other three simply hit the deck.

But because their colleague's body prevented them from closing the hatchway; the remaining gunmen were caught out in the open. There were compartments on either side of them, but their doors were double locked, to discourage nosy tourists. The gunmen could find no refuge there.

Their only strategy was to produce a massive amount of counterfire and try to get back down the passageway, all while hoping the other Hammer squads would come to their rescue.

Meanwhile, Starr and Harvey had the two Super-89s and the open hatch to use as cover. What followed was one of the most intense gun battles of Starr's career.

It went on for two minutes, nonstop. With Kalashnikov-Kissed AR-8/9s firing on both sides, the tracer streaks were going in all directions. The gang members doubled their efforts to throw up a wall of lead while trying to maneuver their way out of the predicament. But

Starr and Harvey kept the pressure up by firing whenever the gang members weren't. The noise was tremendous.

In the middle of all this, Starr's phone rang.

But it wasn't Bull.

It was Angel.

"I think I've got this marriage name thing figured out . . ." she said right after hello.

"Tell me—quick," Starr replied, reloading his rifle.

"I went online to a site where couples can combine their last names into one new name. They'll even submit the paperwork to city hall for you to get the name changed officially."

"What would this new name be?"

"The beginning of your name and the last bit of mine . . ."

Starr thought a moment. "So, it would be . . . Star-ski?"

"Yes . . . I think it's romantic.

"Only if you also like the name 'Hutch' . . ."

Angel was too young to understand. She didn't have a clue.

"Just google it, honey. And I've got to go. I love you and see you soon . . ."

"Ditto . . ." she replied. Then she was gone.

Starr turned his attention back to the gun battle.

But something had happened in the meantime. Whether a stray bullet was to blame, or Harvey just happened to get off a lucky shot, but a pipe had been hit just above the gang members and was now leaking a thick red substance into the passageway, covering the three gunmen in goo.

It wasn't aircraft fuel, but rather hydraulic fluid; Starr could smell it. The dense red liquid was used in operating the carrier's massive aircraft elevators.

Hydraulic fluid wasn't combustible, but it was flammable, and it had a sticky quality to it. Two of the gang members were soaked with it and now it was collecting on the deck.

Starr's Super-89 had run through his two banana clips; so had Harvey's. So Starr took out his Glock and fired two rounds into the leaking pipe. Suddenly the dripping became a torrent. His next shot grazed an electrical circuit box, giving him the spark he needed.

Now the blood red fluid was catching fire everywhere.

Starr and Harvey didn't stick around to see what happened next. They dropped the empty Super-89s and started running again, up the stairs and to the flight deck.

Chapter Twenty-Four

The roof of the *Midway* was crowded with vintage warplanes.

A-4 Skyhawks, F-4 Phantoms, F-8 Crusaders. An enormous A-3 Vigilante. Many others, including veteran helicopters, a Huey, a Chinook. There was even a 1950s O-1 Bird Dog, the military cousin to the Piper Cub, as part of a traveling Korean War display.

But there were ghosts up here too. As soon as they reached the hatch leading to the flight deck and Starr stepped outside, he could feel them all around him. The old carrier had served America for a long time, World War II right through Vietnam. A lot of guys who flew from this deck never came back. Others died defending her.

But unlike the miserable souls who'd passed away inside the horrific L-Wing, at least anyone who died up here had the chance to give their life for a worthy cause.

So Starr wasn't feeling uneasy now, taking it all in. Instead, he was feeling pride.

And then his cell phone rang, ruining the moment.

It was Bull.

The boss was apocalyptic, furious that Starr had moved his position yet *again*. Starr was hardly able to say a word, so thick was the torrent of expletives coming his way. Only when Bull stopped to take a breath was Starr able to give him his latest location along with the reason he'd left the gift shop, concluding with a promise not to move anymore.

But then, the line went dead again.

A moment later, they heard a helicopter approaching,

Their rescue would be an airborne extraction; that had been the plan all along.

Part of what had enraged Bull was, by his timeline, his guys had just missed Starr on Exchange Street, then again at the L-Wing. But now they were here, atop the *Midway*, in a place that would not require any kind of violence or fighting in the passageways below. This could be the best kind of airborne removal: quick and painless.

But their rescuers had to see them first. Starr retrieved the near-empty Bic lighter from his boot and flicked it on. If whoever was flying the copter was equipped with Night Vision gear, they might be able to see the weak flame from the lighter.

They'd made their way out onto the flight deck, emerging next to the forward part of the bridge, about two thirds of the way down from the bow. The copter's bright light was heading right at them; it was a Huey, painted all black. Starr flicked the Bic again and waved it back and forth before it died for good.

But the copter's light blinked back twice. The pilots saw them.

Harvey let out a long breath of relief. Their long night was almost over. Yet Starr had a strange thought: If this was an airborne extraction, how would he retrieve his Jag?

The copter was slowing and close to touching down. Its nose light was nearly blinding them.

That's when Starr's intuition started buzzing.

Something was wrong here.

Duck!

He yelled at Harvey: "Get down!"

Suddenly the flight deck in front of them was awash in high caliber gunfire. The copter sped up and went right over their heads, heavy weapons blazing.

"Jesuzz!" Harvey yelled. "I was safer at the jail!"

It was only for Starr's pre-cog that they were still alive. The copter had at least two 50mm cannons in its nose; two quick bursts were enough to tear a hole in the famous carrier's flight deck.

It was Starr's turn to be furious. Their rescue force had just mistaken them for the bad guys and had opened up, desecrating one of the country's floating treasures.

Typical of how the night was going.

Now they watched as the copter went into a tight 180-degree turn.

It was coming back.

Chapter Twenty-Five

Starr and Harvey hustled down the deck, running about 50 feet before sliding under the biggest plane on display: the A-3 Vigilante bomber.

The rakish 1960s-era jet was a monster when it came to carrier ops and twice the size of the smaller fighter jets parked nearby. Best of all, it had long loping wings. If there was a good place to hide up here, this might be it.

The copter passed over again. Firing straight down, it hit a half dozen aircraft nearby, more desecration, but missing the A-3 entirely. Starr angrily tried to get his phone to work. He had to call Bull and tell him they were being fired on by their own rescuers.

And he actually got the thing to work. He heard a dial tone and punched in Bull's number. As soon as Bull answered, Starr started screaming "Blue on blue!" code that the friendlies were shooting at them—and not the bad guys.

But after shouting the warning three times and waiting for Bull's response, he heard . . . nothing.

There was dead silence for a few seconds—then the phone connection was lost for good.

An eerie silence came over the old warship.

The helicopter didn't come back; Starr prayed hard that Bull had gotten through to them.

But the chopper *had* made quite a racket in its brief appearance—and attracted a lot of attention from their pursuers. In his mind's eye, Starr could see every gang member still alive aboard the carrier, taking the ladderways two at a time, heading for the flight deck.

Then, a voice . . .

"Hey lawyer!" someone in the darkness called out, their voice echoing down the flight deck. "Give it up now and you can walk away. We just need to recover the fugitive."

But Harvey was violently shaking his head no.

"They'll kill us both as soon as they see us," he whispered urgently to Starr.

Starr almost laughed at him. "Do you really think I'd quit now?"

Before Harvey could reply, streams of red tracer fire were suddenly ricocheting all around them. The gunmen were firing *underneath* the wings of the display aircraft, the crimson phosphorescent rounds madly ping-ponging their way down the deck.

This showed the gang members were getting impatient. They were going to clear the deck with continuous shooting until they either hit or trapped someone.

But it made for a major light display—*not* standard special forces tactics.

And this part of it *was* strange. Because Starr and Harvey heard a large *boom!* come from behind them. Suddenly the sky was awash in reds, blues and greens. More loud bangs followed. They both thought for a moment, then groaned.

"Friday Night Pops . . ." they said at once.

They looked over their shoulders towards Broadway Pier. Every Friday night the local merchants sponsored a display of patriotic-themed fireworks. They were always big, bright and noisy.

They were also happening not a quarter mile away. The tracer firing on the *Midway*'s deck could easily be confused as part of the larger Pops pyrotechnics.

To Starr's bad luck, it was the perfect cover for all the noise the gang members were making.

He caught a glimpse of their assailants now, down the deck, not 100 feet away. They were walking in two lines abreast, six guys in each line. The first line was shooting, and the second line was looking for casualties.

The final hunt was on.

Chapter Twenty-Six

Starr had rarely been in a tighter spot.

Movement was impossible for them on the flight deck. While the A-3's landing gear was big enough to hide behind, the plane's huge wing and fuselage just gave the fiery rounds coming their way more room to bounce around in.

The Friday Night Pops were at full throttle now, the noise and shock waves rippling across the harbor, masking the crackling tracer barrages sweeping the deck.

And at least two of the gunmen were getting very close to them.

Counter tactics . . . quick.

Starr checked his Glock. Just three rounds left, the hated unlucky three. He slipped off the safety and then with Harvey watching him, he laid flat out on the deck, the pistol in front of him.

Suddenly the gang members stopped firing. Their tactic had been an overall success; while they'd found no bodies, this just meant they had Starr and Harvey trapped in a manageable kill box with nowhere to run.

One of the gunmen appeared at the nose of the big plane. Starr and Harvey remained frozen. The pair of black combat boots came closer. Starr laid his pistol flat on the deck.

Closer.

Starr wrapped his finger around the trigger.

Closer.

The boots passed by the A-3's lowered flap, moving this way and that, their owner scanning the deck around him.

Starr moved the pistol a half inch to the left.

The gang member cleared the flap and now Starr could see him from the waist down. He was carrying a Super-89 with a triple-rig of banana clips.

Closer . . .

Starr took a deep breath—and held it.

The man's left boot came so close now it almost stepped on Starr's free hand.

A giant firework went off an instant later—and Starr squeezed the trigger.

The huge round blew off the man's foot, boot and all. His first response was to take four violent hops to his right, suddenly one-footed and swearing mightily. Then he lost his balance—and went over the side.

He screamed all the way down before hitting the asphalt pier, his cries ending with a disturbing crack.

Two bullets left.

Starr was picking up his pistol when he saw a red phosphorus light coming right at him.

Put your hand up . . .

Even to Starr himself, it felt like the tracer hit his left wrist before deflecting off at a strange angle. Still he managed to raise his pistol and shoot his attacker in the groin. The man fell at Harvey's feet, dead before he hit the deck. A perfect shot . . .

Harvey had once been a field medic. He tore off his orange prison top, intent on wrapping it around Starr's wrist to stem the massive bleeding.

But Starr wasn't bleeding. His wrist was intact, he still had both hands—and he'd just gunned down the guy who nearly killed him, all without missing a beat.

Starr was as shocked as Harvey. He looked at his sleeve and saw a dull glow of pink phosphorescence covered the cuff. The incendiary bullet must have skimmed the brass button on his jacket cuff and pinged away. That was the only explanation.

Only one thing was for certain. Had he not raised his hand when he did, the bullet would have shattered his skull.

By the light of the next big firework, Harvey looked over at him and gasped: "Who the fuck *are* you?"

Starr brushed the red glow from his jacket cuff and tightened it again.

"I really don't know," he replied.

Chapter Twenty-Seven

The fireworks continued.

The near-blinding explosions sent even larger shock waves rumbling across the bay, powerful enough to shake the other airplanes on the carrier's deck.

Unaware that two of their brothers had been iced, the gang members were still approaching Starr and Harvey from three sides, reloading their Super-89s.

But between the crazily-gyrating shadows and the earsplitting sonic boom-like blasts, Starr and Harvey were able to crawl out from under the A-3 and down to a gun porch. Running low but as fast as they could, they made their way another 100 feet to the stern of the carrier.

Starr knew the gang members would eventually catch them if they stayed up top. But going back to running through the old ship wasn't much of an option either. Two more truckloads of gang members had just arrived down on the pier and were in the process of flooding onto the ship.

This left a single course of action. They couldn't rely on promises of rescue any longer. Though it meant defying Bull *again*, Starr knew they had to get off the ship on their own. And there was really only one way left to do it.

They climbed back up on the flight deck near the Korean War display. The old Cessna was in perfect shape, a true collectible. It had been about a year since Starr last flew a plane; but he wasn't planning on going very far.

Harvey climbed into the small propeller plane's passenger seat; Starr slid behind the controls. The keys were still in the ignition.

The Friday Night Pops were beginning their grand finale. Starr waited until a particularly loud barrage exploded, took a deep breath . . . and gave the keys a twist.

For Angel, he whispered.

The old warhorse's engine turned over.

He gunned the engine, stepped off the brakes and off they went. Straight down the middle of the deck, gaining speed. The gang members were so unaware what was happening, the plane's wing hit two of them, sending them flying. But suddenly the top of the ship was laced with tracer fire, all of it following the tiny airplane as it sped down the flight deck.

But it was too late.

Reaching the end of the carrier's deck, Starr pulled back on the controls, lifted the nose and they were airborne.

Chapter Twenty-Eight

It was just another weird chapter in Starr's life that the same bus driver who had picked up Harvey, soaking wet, the day before when Starr was chasing him, now picked them both up, both soaking wet, both without any money—and did so without batting an eye.

Starr had crash landed the Cessna in about 20 feet of water off the South Avenue Beach. They'd both jumped from the airplane five seconds before it went in. They hit the water at the same time, Starr actually touching the bottom of the bay before making his way back up to the surface.

Harvey was already swimming towards the beach; Starr was close behind. They could hear shouting and other noises coming from the carrier's deck, now far away. And the Friday Night Pops were still going off. And the plane was a total wreck.

They'd hopped on the bus and Starr decreed now was the time to go to the Navy Base. He breathed a sigh of relief when he finally sat down.

He tried to call Bull, hoping to report this sudden turn of events . . . when he felt something cold against his right temple. It was the barrel of his .357. Just one huge round left.

Harvey was pointing it at him.

"Really?" Starr asked him, genuinely surprised. "After all we've been through?'

"I'll still plead guilty and take my punishment," Harvey told him. "But I have to see Mary one last time . . ."

The bus driver wordlessly left them off at the corner of Hillside and California Ave. It was a short walk to Funny Bones from there.

To his credit, Harvey did not hold the gun on Starr the whole time. Starr had silently agreed to just going along with it. He'd been through so much already this night—explosions, gunfights, a plane crash—a trip to Funny Bones before Harvey went back to jail would be no big deal.

It was now 1:00 a.m.

The morgue attendant was just arriving for his shift when Starr and Harvey appeared at the door.

They were still soaking wet and were both covered with cuts, bumps and burn marks. They didn't look much better than some of the morgue's occupants. The attendant was understandably confused, so Starr tried to explain what they were doing there.

"Do you recall yesterday when we had a bit of . . . gender confusion with one of the departed?"

The attendant nodded. "How could I forget?"

It was then that Harvey chose to show the attendant that he was holding the .357 to Starr's back.

"So, anyway," Starr went on. "My friend here would just like to pay his respects to that particular person and we're in agreement that it can happen painlessly. OK?"

The attendant's eyes were focused on the gun. "You bet. No problem."

He pulled out Mary's drawer and then stepped away.

"Take your time," Starr told Harvey, but he knew the Marine captain couldn't hear him. He was in another world.

Starr joined the attendant a few feet away. The man was shaking.

"Believe me I was just as surprised as anyone," the attendant whispered to him. "I didn't know she was a tranny until I pulled the drawer open for you guys."

Once again Starr heard the needle scratching the record.

Something didn't make sense.

He took two steps back and chanced a look at the morgue's computer. It was showing the daily log. Mary's entry was at the bottom of the screen. The line asking the sex of the deceased was blank. Not unusual. She was covered when found, so the coroner's drivers left the sex ID to the morgue.

But if the coroner's people didn't know Mary's secret, and neither did the morgue attendant . . . how did Bull?

Starr saw it just before it happened. The morgue's door swung wide open and standing there was the massive hulk of Bull Parades. He had a Glock in his hand. He fired one round which caught Harvey in the chest. The Marine captain collapsed immediately. A second shot caught the morgue attendant in just about the same place.

Then Bull pointed the gun at Starr.

"You're pretty dumb for someone who has ESP," Bull told him.

Starr didn't understand.

Bull just shook his head. "Fucking kids they let in these days," he said.

He stepped inside the morgue and closed the door.

"Every time I called you—on the street, at the L-Wing, on the ship—I was giving your position to my friends in the Pier 44 gang. They were going crazy trying to track you down, along with your date."

It took about a nanosecond for it all to be clear in Starr's mind. But as it turned out, it was a few nanoseconds too late.

"Hey look, I tried to steer you off the gun case," Bull told him. "And I ordered you off the Dick Chick case too. But you wouldn't leave it alone."

Starr was astonished. Bull was a tough guy and a tough boss, but he never suspected him of being a traitor.

"Are you so worried about your pension that you have to make money like this?" Starr asked him.

Bull just laughed. "You know this country treats its veterans like shit. What can I expect when I get out? Trying to feed two ex-wives and myself? Certainly not what I deserve. So it was either live like a pauper—or this."

Starr suddenly saw a disturbing image of Bull putting two big rounds in his chest. It was one vision he didn't want to see come true.

So he rushed him.

He hit the huge man with a running block, knocking the gun from his hand, but doing little else.

Bull picked him up and threw him across the room; he landed hard against the freezer door. By the time the stars left Starr's eyes, Bull was standing over him. This time he picked him up by the knees and hurled him into a table full of morgue tools.

Starr did his best to roll off the broken glass and twisted metal, but Bull grabbed him once again. But this time, before he could throw him, Starr jammed a surgeon's scalpel into Bull's bulging neck. It immediately produced a gush of blood . . . but it didn't slow down his boss one bit.

He threw Starr against the hard marble wall and then retrieved his gun. He was ready to deliver the coup de grace.

"I'm sorry kid," Bull said. "This whole thing blew up tonight and some of the other guys were killed, so there's no way I can let you go."

Starr could see Bull's finger starting to pull the trigger when suddenly there was a loud buzzing and then sickly *crack!* A piece of the Bull's skull came flying off and hit the ceiling. Bull was stunned. Blood was suddenly pouring all over him. He turned to reveal a battered, dying Harvey, holding an electric bone saw.

The two men wavered for a moment, but then collapsed at Starr's feet. In seconds, both were dead on the morgue's floor, the bone saw still buzzing away in Harvey's hand.

Chapter Twenty-Nine

It was noon when Starr fell in the door to his apartment.

He hadn't been here in more than 24 hours—it seemed like 24 years.

Angel was waiting for him. She was wearing a plaid shirt, jeans and a white baseball cap, the latest in casual chic. He, on the other hand, was a mess and looked it. But she was just glad he was home in one piece.

She took off his jacket and sat him down in a kitchen chair. She handed him two beers, just to save time. He downed the first one in five gulps. Then he opened the second and began to drink more slowly. He was beyond exhausted. Though he'd been able to recover the Jag once the surviving gang members had been rounded up with the help of the SDPD and the Highway Patrol, he'd barely kept his eyes open driving home.

Angel took off his baseball cap and rubbed his weary head. "Should I even ask what happened?"

He just shook his head no and slugged the beer.

"How about the short version?" she prodded him gently.

"Short version? I just got promoted."

She stared back at him "What happened to Bull?"

"He's . . . dead," Starr said, finding the words hard to say. "And the taxpayers won't have to pay for a trial in the Dick Chick case. Harvey killed him and he killed Harvey."

Angel was shocked to hear all this. But she was also resilient.

"Bull always struck me as a weirdo—but he didn't deserve to die."

Starr took her hand and told her: "Yes he did. He was a bad character. Really up to no good."

"So the case is over?"

"Both of them. They're rounding up the rest of Pier 44 guys and we now know the reason for Mary's murder."

She helped him up, got him through the wormhole and into her bedroom. He lay down on the bed.

"I'm so sorry now I didn't go to Puffs with you," she said, stroking his head again.

"Don't worry about it," he told her tiredly. "It didn't matter. In the end they were just people. Harvey, the gang members, the regulars at Puffs. Good or bad, just people doing what people do."

She snuggled up to him. "But who knew it would end like this?"

"Not me, that's for sure," he said. "That's why it's such a shame about Mary. She wasn't killed because of who she was, but for what she knew."

Book Two

Abrams Island

Chapter One

Christmas Eve had come to Old Seabury, Massachusetts.

The small coastal town on Boston's South Shore was aglow with holiday lights on every street. Elegant decorations were hanging from businesses and houses along its picturesque bayside waterfront. The church steeple was wrapped in pine roping.

Sleepy now, Old Seabury was popular in the summer. Ten thousand residents during July and August—just a thousand the rest of the year. Lots of nice beaches, lots of fishing, seafood, bars and clam shacks. When you went on the state's tourism board's website, a picture of the town's lighthouse was the first thing you saw.

About a mile across the bay was Old Seabury Island, a favorite of the very well-heeled. Long and narrow, covered with wetlands and dunes, it boasted a large nature preserve at one end, white sandy cliffs at the other. At its center was a tiny village containing a handful of businesses and two dozen oceanfront cottages, all with price tags north of ten million.

A meandering causeway ran through the town's marshes leading to the Old Seabury Bridge. Passing over an unnamed river, the ancient wooden span connected the south end of the island to the mainland.

But taking the bridge was considered the long way around. In the summer, most people used the town's small ferry to get to the island.

In the winter, when the island emptied out except for a few die-hards, the bridge was hardly used.

A giant blizzard was coming.

Two immense polar vortexes were predicted to collide over Boston around midnight creating a double bombogenesis. Ninety-five mile-an-hour winds and 48 inches of snow were in the forecast, with power outages and road closures sure to follow. From Connecticut to Maine, all of New England was waiting for what had already been dubbed the Christmas Mega-Storm.

The snow started falling on Old Seabury around 5:00 p.m. It picked up quickly over the next hour. By six, the wind was at full howl and the snow was blowing sideways off the ocean. Businesses closed, church services were cancelled, plowing began. The town hunkered down, prepared to ride out the massive nor'easter.

Then, at exactly 6:05, an explosion shook the tiny community.

The 911 calls came pouring in. People could see smoke rising from the marshes south of town. One man armed with infrared binoculars reported the old wooden bridge had just blown up. Others confirmed the bridge was on fire.

Just as Old Seabury's tiny police force was coming to grips with this, a second explosion rocked the town. The McMansion at 45 Water Street down by the bay had been blown to bits, a huge blast leveling it completely.

The fire department arrived in minutes; they pulled the owner from the wreckage. Dan Peabody, a prominent attorney, was rushed to a nearby hospital in grave condition.

Witnesses told police they'd seen some kind of fiery object shoot up from the island, fly over the bay and hit the big house.

Later on, witnesses would say a similar object blew up the Old Seabury Bridge.

Chapter Two

The Massachusetts Turnpike closed from Lee to Boston in anticipation of the super storm.

The snowplows were out in force, but only one car dared to drive the perilous roadway. It was a 1989 Jaguar XJS coupe. Lt. Chris Starr was at the wheel.

Angel was with him; they were heading to Boston where her parents lived. It was time for their annual Christmas bash, a party so good, they'd driven across country just to attend.

It had been smooth sailing most of the way, but then they hit the northeast and the weather began to deteriorate.

This was not a problem though. On a hunch, Starr had put extra wide Pirelli XVV tires on the Jag before departing the Coast. Now he was able to cruise along at 60 mph despite the heavy precipitation, the bulbous sneakers keeping the car stuck to the pavement and under control.

Except for the snowplows, they were the only ones on the highway.

"I'm pretending we're royalty or something," Angel said. "And the plows are clearing the way, just for us."

"Isn't that just another way of saying 'we're the only two nuts out here in this weather'?" Starr asked.

She shook her head in mild disgust. "Remember that the next time you want me to 'pretend' something."

He reached for his old cellphone and held it up where she could see it.

He said: "Three . . . two . . . one . . . *now!*"

The phone rang on cue. She pretended to yawn.

He flipped open the phone. The call was from an old friend, Jim Cook, police chief of Old Seabury, Mass. He knew Starr was visiting the area for the holidays.

They had an intense ten-minute conversation, long enough for Starr to get off the Mass Pike and onto the streets of Boston. The topic was so strange Starr found himself exclaiming: "Are you kidding me?" over and over. Angel couldn't imagine what they were talking about.

The call ended just as they arrived at Angel's parents' brownstone in Back Bay Boston—all 15 rooms of it—with views of the Charles River, Boston Harbor and the ocean beyond. Covered with white lights and garlands it looked like the cover of a Christmas card.

"You're leaving me, aren't you?" she asked him as they pulled up.

"A friend needs a favor," Starr said with a shrug. "Jim Cook, down in Old Seabury."

"But you'll miss the party . . ." she said.

Starr knew Angel's family well. This party would last three days, maybe four. Factor in the mega storm and it might go a week.

"I'll miss the first night, that's it," he told her. "Ask your dad to save me a little scotch, the blue-label stuff. I'll make up for it when I get back."

Angel was used to this. She didn't get upset whenever it happened, but she did worry about him.

Starr parked the Jag, ran around to her door and let her out. They walked up the stairs to the townhouse's front door where they hugged and kissed.

"Be careful please? For me?" she asked him.

"I will . . ."

"Especially in this weather."

"I'm on it. See you tomorrow."

They kissed again, then he ran back down the stairs and into the swirling snow. Jumping in the Jag, he wheeled around and headed for Route 95 South.

Old Seabury was only a half hour away.

Chapter Three

Starr pulled up to the Old Seabury police station just before 7:00 p.m.

Power was out in parts of the town by now and the blowing snow had grown even worse. The roar from of the ocean nearby sounded like thunder. Visibility was zero.

Cook met Starr at the station's front door. He looked like a trim, well-groomed Santa Claus. They'd known each other for a long time. Cookie was a good guy and a good cop.

He hustled Starr inside; a cup of coffee was waiting for him on Cook's desk. Starr loaded it up with a dozen packets of sugar and almost as many artificial creamers.

Lined up on the desk in front of him were five cell phones.

All of them were ringing.

"The regular land line phones are down," Cook explained, swigging his own cup of Joe. "But somehow our cells are still working . . ."

Starr had a sudden thought: *Not for long . . .*

The next instant, all five phones went dead. Cook banged them on the desktop, two at a time, trying to revive them, but to no avail.

A deputy came in from the storm, fighting to close the door behind him.

"Bad news, Cookie," he reported. "The wind finally got to the cell tower. I just saw it go over. It fell across St. Mary's, broke in two and hit the manger scene out front. It cut off the baby Jesus' head . . ."

"That can't be good," Starr said, stirring his coffee with his finger.

"So we can't talk to *anybody* on the phone?" Cook asked the deputy.

The man shook his head. "Everything's down. Regular phones and cells. And forget about our radios. They stopped working an hour ago."

With some exasperation, Cook pulled on a winter parka and handed a spare to Starr.

"Want to look at the scene?" he asked the Navy detective.

"Please, lead on," Starr replied.

They went out to Cook's cruisier and were off into the stormy night. The chief updated Starr as they drove along battling the wind and snow.

The destroyed mansion. The bridge. The strange things seen before the house blew up. Cook admitted he was hoping that a natural gas line was to blame for destroying the mansion. But that sure wouldn't explain the bridge.

They arrived at the scene on Water Street. Cook's entire force was out here now, manning a perimeter.

Starr was astonished. The house wasn't just destroyed, it had been absolutely flattened. The area around it was steaming, clouds of hot smoke were climbing into the massive storm. But there was no fire because there was nothing left to burn. It was almost surreal.

They got out of the cruiser and studied the damage up close. Starr looked over the debris, then picked up some of the snowy soot and tasted it.

"Jessuz," he swore.

"What is it?" Cook wanted to know.

Starr put the soot to his tongue again "This is from a very high explosive. Maybe part of an artillery round."

Cook looked at him, his face turning white.

"An artillery round?" he said. "Do you hear what you're saying . . .?"

"I can't believe I'm even *thinking* it," Starr replied. "But this wasn't a gas explosion or even dynamite. And you said people saw something in the air heading this way just before the explosion?"

He turned and looked towards the island across the bay. He could hardly see it in the gales of snow.

"There's only one explanation." he went on. "Someone on that island has a big gun capable of firing high explosive rounds. One shell was enough to obliterate this house and it sounds like the bridge before it."

Cook was still in disbelief. He'd been expecting something crazy. But not *this* crazy.

"I mean really, Chris? What kind of artillery could be out there?"

"The homemade kind, maybe?" Starr said, fighting to be heard over the storm. "The Syrian rebels fought for so long, they learned how to build their own surface to surface missiles. Completely DIY, steered them with cell phones, amazingly accurate."

"But here?" Cook said. "This has got to be the most unlikely place in the world for a terrorist attack."

"I know," Starr replied, once again looking back at the thin strip of land still barely visible on the horizon. "But, believe me, something like that is happening."

Chapter Four

Thirty minutes later, four pickup trucks arrived at the Old Seabury ferry dock.

Four men got out; each was wearing foul weather gear. Each was carrying a hunting rifle.

Starr was waiting for them.

It was now 8:00 p.m. and the situation in the small town had worsened rapidly.

Just before the phones went down, Cook made an urgent call to the Massachusetts State Police telling them what little he knew about the twin explosions—but he had no idea if the right people even received his message. He'd sent his one last spare deputy out to drive Route 95, 25 miles north to Weymouth, Mass., the site of a state police barracks. At best it would take him at least two hours just to get there. That's how bad the storm had become.

But time was at a premium. Someone had to get over to the island now and find out what was going on. Cook and his small police force were already overtasked with evacuating *everyone* in Old Seabury and taking them to the old fallout shelter at the Vo-tech high school just outside town. Getting civilians out of harm's way was the

OSPD's number one priority; trying to get their phones working again was also high on the list.

So Starr volunteered to go over to the island—by ferry.

These four men would be going with him. They were friends of Chief Cook, all in their late 30s, all with some law enforcement or military training.

They were Brothers Jim and Andy Taylor, both big, strapping guys, both part time deputies and two Army veterans, Rich Jackson, lean and pumped, and Joel Coward, who had a bookworm air about him.

None of them had any idea what to expect ahead, Starr included. His pre-cog abilities hadn't been any help since he'd arrived in Old Seabury. He'd tried hard to get something to click, all while knowing it didn't work like that. The magic came to him and went away when it wanted to; and it didn't take requests.

So he'd drawn up a very loose plan, with each step doubting he could ever put it into action.

They had to get to the island, but the complications weren't just the roaring wind and heavy snow. Problem number one was the town's summer ferry. It was tiny. Just 30 feet long and 10 feet wide, big enough to carry two cars or one truck, but that was it. Designed for fair weather sailing only, its top speed was eight knots, it had no navigation gear and its communication link was a walkie-talkie with corroded batteries.

Problem two: if they somehow made it to the island, the little group would in effect become a search party, looking for whatever was bombarding Old Seabury. The island was narrow, but it was also five miles long, impossible to search on foot in this weather.

Starr's plan included bringing one of Old Seabury's snowplows with them, something to get them around the island in the worsening storm. But because the town's newer plows were working all out already, the only apparatus Cook could spare was the town's long-retired 1955 Oshkosh six-wheel, five-ton Snow King.

It was a massive vehicle. Giant V-plow in front with two wing plows on the sides, six gigantic tires, a huge tinted windshield, and an 18-inch searchlight operated from the passenger side seat. Its back bed was filled with road salt for ballast and it did have a double cab, meaning the five of them could all fit inside. And luckily the heater still worked.

But it was an antique and it looked it.

The Taylor brothers pulled the small ferry out of its enclosed slip and started its cranky diesel engine.

Because the vessel loaded from the front, they had to back the old snowplow on board. Jackson was a drivers' ed teacher in real life—but it took him four tries to get the plow onto the fiercely bobbing ferry. The truck weighed so much, Starr was sure they would sink right there at the dock. But while the hull did go low in the water, somehow the ferry stayed afloat.

Deputy Andy took up station behind the boat's steering wheel; he'd worked on the ferry as a kid and knew a little about running it. The rest of the team lashed the big plow to the deck with chains and ropes.

After making sure everything on board was secure, Deputy Andy eased the tiny vessel out into the turbulent bay.

It got rough right away. The water was so churned up, giant waves began crashing onto the deck immediately. Then the ferry began oscillating, violently rocking from side to side and allowing even more seawater to pour in.

A minute went by, but the waves only grew bigger and the ferry would not stop rocking. The big snowplow began to fight against its chains. If one snapped and the truck shifted too far one way or another, the ferry would go right over. And even with life jackets, it would be tough to survive the freezing water.

Deputy Andy increased their speed and the ferry settled down a bit, but they knew they were in for a soaking, blowing, anxiety-ridden crawl. The wind became more ferocious the farther out they went and with the snow absolutely blinding, a green channel marker just off the island's dock was the only navigational guide they could find. It was all Andy could do to keep the dull emerald glow in sight.

It took more than thirty minutes just to get halfway across the bay. The ferry's depth finder, just about the only panel instrument still working, indicated they were above the bay's deepest part; 55 feet to the rocky bottom. This made what happened next even more frightening.

Starr saw it coming two seconds before it appeared. A streak of blazing red light rising up from the island and heading right for them. It looked like . . . fireworks.

Friday Night Pops . . .

Starr had just enough time to yell: "Hang on!"

There was a tremendous crash not twenty feet off their starboard side. The explosion was so powerful, the ferry began to capsize for real.

Deputy Andy pulled them back from the brink by burying the throttle and spinning the ship's wheel to port. The ferry slammed back down onto the waves, shaking from bow to stern. But then another blast hit off their port side, this one even closer. It rocked the ferry so badly the snowplow snapped one of its chains and started sliding to the right. Gallons of seawater rushed in. They were seconds from going down.

"I think someone is trying to tell us something!" Coward shouted over the storm.

"Yeah, like get the hell out of here!" Deputy Jim yelled back.

The third explosion actually saved them. It landed off starboard and the resulting wave counteracted the round that had just hit before it. The ferry shook once again right down to its rivets, blowing out what was left of the bridge's windows. But the tiny ship somehow righted itself and the plow stopped thrashing about.

And then once again, all they could hear was the roar of the storm around them. They held their breaths, waiting for another barrage, but nothing ever came.

Whatever destroyed the McMansion on Water Street and the Old Seabury Bridge had just shot at them—and somehow they'd survived. And they were all shaken. But the idea of turning around never came up.

Instead Deputy Andy pushed the throttles back to two-thirds and they resumed plowing through the rough seas, slowly getting closer to the island.

Chapter Five

Fifteen minutes later, the ferry passed what was left of the Old Seabury Bridge.

Whoever destroyed the wooden span couldn't have placed their explosive more perfectly. There was a little bit of debris, and a few scattered fires about, but that was it.

Already buried under tons of unplowed snow, the causeway leading to the island was now cut in half—and would remain that way for a long time.

The ferry chugged past the green channel marker. They were getting close now. Though they didn't want to make themselves a target again, they were forced to illuminate their deck lights so they could find the island's ferry dock. It was little more than a pier, a fuel pump and a Coke machine located across from Center Street, home to the island's tiny village.

Once the landing was spotted in the blowing snow, Starr and Deputy Jim made their way down to the bow of the ferry, each carrying a docking loop. They had to snag one of the pier posts and pull the ferry into the dock, not easy to do even on the calmest days. If they failed, one of them would have to jump in the water, swim to the dock and climb up top and have the other man try to throw the loop to him. Neither one of them wanted to go with that option.

But it didn't make any difference because another high-explosive shell changed everything.

Once more, Starr saw the sizzling warhead rocketing through the storm two seconds before it hit. Its target was the dock itself. It hit the structure with a gigantic *boom!*

Although the ferry was still about 300 feet out, the explosion's backwash nearly capsized them yet again. But it was the rain of debris that proved most dangerous. The old dock was made of wood and a lot of it, hurled into the air by the blast, began falling onto the ferry, all of it on fire. Suddenly flames were sweeping across the deck, whipped up by the storm's 90 mph winds.

Starr reached for the bridge's fire extinguisher, only to find it was no bigger than a tall can of Bud. The entire front part of the ferry was aflame; this little thing wouldn't put a dent in the inferno.

But then his antennas went up. Something was coming—not an explosive, but something just as dramatic.

Again, he had just enough time to tell everyone to hang on.

An instant later, another mammoth wave crashed across the bow, soaking the deck and putting out all the fires.

This all took place in a matter of seconds. Once again, the team members were part euphoric, part dumbstruck, knowing they were lucky to still be alive.

"I can't believe that just happened!" Deputy Jim yelled over the storm.

Starr wiped the seawater and soot from his face.

"I can't believe *any* of this is happening," he whispered.

But then a new problem . . .

They weren't on fire anymore—but the ferry dock was gone. There was nowhere for them to tie up.

Now what? They could return to where the old bridge had stood. They might be able to jump ship and get up to the causeway, but the grade was too steep to bring the plow. And depending on which side of the bridge they picked, they could either walk onto the island from there—or go back to Old Seabury. Those seemed to be their only options.

"There's a boat ramp at the south end of the island," Deputy Andy said suddenly. "Maybe we can drive off down there . . ."

"There's also a jetty down there," Brother Jim said. "If we hit that, we'll sink like a stone."

For Starr, the thought of beaching the battered ferry in the howling superstorm sounded daunting at best. He looked to Coward and Jackson, the Army vets. "What do you guys think?"

"I'm not a sailor," Coward said right away.

"But it might be better than trying to turn around and go back," Jackson added. "We'd be back in that gun's sights the whole way."

Starr begged his pre-cog instincts to guide him, but it was still no soap. Two hours ago, he'd been in his nice warm car, zooming along with Angel, ready to celebrate Christmas.

Now . . . he was out here, in the middle of all this.

He thought a few more moments and then said: "Okay, screw it—let's give it a try . . ."

Chapter Six

It took another half hour to get to the south end of the island.

This is where the cliffs were. Also, the island side of the now severed causeway started here. Close by was the jetty and the boat ramp. But all of this was obscured by the storm and the dark.

They received another unexpected assist, though, courtesy of more wild atmospherics going on around them. Because by this time, on top of everything else, it had started thundering and lightning.

"In the middle of a freaking blizzard," Jackson exclaimed, the flashes lighting up the swirling snow above them. "*That's* how you know you're in New England."

But it was a convenient flash of lightning that lit up the jetty just enough for them to brace for impact.

The bow hit first, slamming into the jagged rocks and causing the ferry to lurch upwards, do a violent pivot to the left and then come back down with a great *bang!* But incredibly, it landed right on top of the boat ramp. The snowplow broke through the rest of its chains, crashed through the ferry's locked gate and toppled onto the ramp as well, wheels up.

The team didn't stop to question their astonishing good luck. They grabbed their weapons, scrambled off the ferry and piled into the plow. Jackson slid behind the wheel and cranked the old engine; it turned over on the third try. A cheer went up. Jackson needed Starr's help to push the floor shift into gear and then they spent the next half-minute churning up layers of crusty sea ice covering the ramp, praying to get some traction. Finally, the truck's big wheels took hold and they started moving forward.

Driving their way through the foot-deep water, they reached the frozen beach, went up and over a picnic table and found themselves on the island's narrow access road.

It was little more than a wide path that crept along the bayside of the island, but it went north—the direction they wanted to go.

Jackson lowered the truck's giant V-blade and they began plowing their way towards the middle of the island. But before they got more than a hundred feet, they heard another, even louder noise over the roar of the storm. It was the ferry coming apart out on the jetty. Battered by the waves and the rocks, it broke up quickly, scattering its remains to the sea.

"I guess that means we're swimming home," Deputy Jim said.

Chapter Seven

It took them another half hour to drive the two mile long access road.

Tall sand dunes were on their right, the storm-tossed bay to their left. The dunes would have been perfect wind blocks—except the blizzard was blowing in the other direction now. Nor'easters moved in circular fashion and at the moment the 90-mph gusts were coming from the south, strong enough to shake the old massive snowplow.

Every few minutes Starr would punch Cook's number into his ancient cell phone, hoping by some miracle that mobile phone service had been restored in Old Seabury and the chief would pick up. He got a busy signal every time. But he kept trying.

They came upon the first sign of habitation about a quarter mile from the island's center. A row of five fishing shacks, set back from the shoreline and protected by thickets of plumbush trees. Only one shack had a light on. The rest were boarded up for the winter.

Jackson brought the huge rig to a slushy stop and Starr and Deputy Jim jumped out. Their shoulders dipped against the violently blowing snow, they made their way to the shack's front door.

Starr had barely knocked when the door flew open. A shotgun was waiting for him—a double barrel Remington 562 held by a small, wiry man easily in his 80s.

"Trick or treat?" Deputy Jim said.

Starr took possession of the shotgun, quickly but gently pushing it aside and then twisting its owner's wrists until he could hold it no more. But the old guy was just protecting his home and Starr wasn't there to embarrass him.

"We're the good guys," Starr told him, handing back the shotgun, this time barrels down. He flashed his Navy ID and asked. "What's going on out here, besides the storm?"

The man pulled them inside and closed the door. The shack's walls were covered with dozens of fishing rods. Fishhooks hung from the ceiling. A wood stove was roaring away in one corner, heating it all.

The man introduced himself as Norman.

"All kinds of crap happening," he told them excitedly. "This mutha of a storm. Big explosions up near the center. I thought they were thunder until I saw one. Like the biggest fireworks ever, and . . ."

Only then did he look his two visitors up and down. Covered with ice head to toe, they looked like they were melting.

"How the hell did you guys get out here?" he asked them.

"We took the ferry," Starr said.

The man's eyes brightened. "The ferry's here? So I can get off the island?"

Starr and Deputy Jim exchanged troubled looks.

"Not right away," Starr said. "We're here to look into those fireworks. Could you tell where they were coming from?"

"The first two looked like they came from just around the center."

"How many did you see?"

"Easily a half dozen. The rest looked like they came from further up the island, like near the nature preserve."

Starr's heart sank. He'd never considered that there was more than one big DIY gun out here. Now they might be facing at least two.

Norman went on: "After all that commotion, I just locked myself in here. I'm the only one out here this time of year—and that's why I got my gun out."

He took a breath, then asked: "So what *is* going on? Do you know?"

Starr just shook his head.

"Not yet," he said.

Chapter Eight

They squeezed Norman into the back seat of the plow and started moving again.

The old guy began talking right away. He'd lived on the island almost all of his 84 years. Except for the Korean War, and a brief marriage, his life had been all about fishing and running fishing boats.

He'd seen the island turn from a small, friendly family vacation place to a haven for millionaires and billionaires. Massive homes built. Asphalt roads laid down. Everything got more expensive. Norman knew all was lost when they opened a candle shop down at the center.

"This place has been going crazy for years," Norman concluded. "I'm not surprised it's blowing itself up."

They continued plowing their way through the waist deep, high drifting snow. Meanwhile, Deputy Andy explained the situation to Norman. The old guy was shocked.

"The bridge is gone?"

"Plus some McMansion on Water Street near the bay," Andy told him.

"So those fireworks were actually some big gun going off?"

"Maybe even a few big guns . . ."

Norman was as puzzled as the rest of them. "But why would someone out here, be shooting at someone over there?"

The plow reached the center of the island.

The remains of the ferry dock were still burning fiercely, whipped-up embers mixing with the blowing snow.

Across from the dock was Center Street and the small, quaint-looking village. A dozen mostly seasonal businesses and a few designed-to-look-rustic cottages. It was a snowy Kinkade painting come to life, but during a blackout.

The power had gone out here long ago, but they could see two buildings with lights flickering inside. Starr groaned. He'd been hoping they'd find this place deserted. Civilians always complicated things.

Jackson pulled the big plow up to the first building showing signs of life. It was a gingerbread cottage with a closed-up t-shirt business attached.

Again, Starr and Deputy Jim jumped out into the blizzard. They knocked three times before the door opened. No shotgun this time—rather three young women were standing on the other side. They'd been huddled around an enormous, scented candle, trying to keep warm. They showed almost no surprise to see Starr and the deputy.

"Are you here to . . . extract us?" one asked, quickly adding: "You know . . . rescue us?"

But neither Starr nor Deputy Jim could reply, not right away. All the three girls were shapely and beautiful. Their hair looked professionally done and they were dressed in high end Nordic clothes.

They looked like . . . models, something Starr knew a little about.

His brain made a quick leap. The girls were here for the winter, keeping their weight down and putting portfolios together, intent on returning to New York in the spring. It was called hibernating in the biz.

"Yes—we're here to rescue you," Starr finally said, flashing his Navy badge. "But we're also looking into other things going on out here. For example, have you been hearing any loud noises?"

The girls bid them in and closed the door.

"Yes, we have," one replied in a slightly undefinable accent, a plus in the modeling world. She was a blonde; her two friends were brunettes. All very, very pretty. "But we also heard some kind of mechanical sound. Like a truck engine, without a muffler."

"Or fire apparatus," one of the brunettes said, also with a slight accent. "You know how loud they can be?"

"Sometimes it seemed like it was right outside," the third girl reported. "But other times it sounded like it was up in the nature preserve."

Only then did Starr see the dozen suitcases stacked near the door. The girls had been expecting an evacuation. They were packed and ready to go.

"So . . ." Blondie asked Starr: "Do you guys have a helicopter?"

Chapter Nine

Jackson had kept the plow's engine running and the cab's heater blasting.

Still there were no complaints when Starr and Deputy Jim shoehorned the three models into the back seat. The blonde introduced herself as Tami; her brunette friends were Tina and Trish. They wound up sharing Norman's lap.

Starr had already given the girls a thumbnail of what was happening. He'd tried to explain it diplomatically: The good news was they would be safer with the team than without them. The bad news: they had to stay with them until they found out what was causing the havoc on the island. The girls were not happy to hear this part, but agreed to soldier on.

The plow started moving again and Starr directed Jackson to the second set of flickering lights further up the street. These were coming from the island's only drinking establishment, the Beachcoma. It was a one story L-shaped building, made of cement blocks and painted mostly yellow. A small dining room on one side, a large bar on the other, it was a holdover from days past and stayed open all year round.

Jackson brought the plow to a noisy halt in the bar's parking lot. There were six cars here, all in the process of being buried by massive snow drifts. Two Mercedes-Benz, two Cadillac Escalades, a BMW and, incomprehensibly, a Lamborghini Centenario Roadster, a million-dollar automobile.

"Not surprised this is where everyone would go in an emergency," Norman said. "Rich or poor . . ."

Starr eyed the collection of high end vehicles, especially the banana-colored Lambo. "I'm guessing mostly rich," he said.

One more time, Starr and Deputy Jim zipped up their parkas, grabbed their weapons and stepped out into the storm.

The winds had increased yet again and the visibility was basically nil. They trudged up to the door of the bar, its summer-themed murals looking surreal in the ferocious snow and gale.

They both had to push on the door to get it open. More or less bursting in, they found a dozen people sitting at the bar, hovering over drinks, dozens of candles providing the light.

Startled at first, the patrons then let out a cheer. Someone yelled: "The cavalry has arrived!"

Starr scanned the room. Six guys, all mid-40s; six wives or girlfriends all in mid-20s. All were dressed in J

Crew winter gear, fashionably matching the high priced cars outside.

These people were also packed and ready to go; a couple dozen suitcases lined one wall. But when the patrons began to gather their things and start for the door, Deputy Jim stopped them in their tracks.

"There's going to be a slight delay in the evacuation," he announced to a collective groan. "Now—has anyone heard any explosions out here?"

They all had.

"We thought it was the waves crashing at first," one guy said. "But our house shook down to the foundation. Five or six times at least. We figured it was something not good, so we tried to convoy off the island—but we found out the bridge was gone. That's when we headed here and hoped someone would come out and get us. Aren't you those people?"

"We are," Starr replied, at the same time knowing there was no way everyone in here could fit in the plow's cab. "But we have to secure the area first."

None of them knew what that meant, so Deputy Jim translated it for them.

"It means you're going to have to stay here until we search the rest of the island."

Chapter Ten

The three girls, Norman and the rest of the team piled out of the plow and into the Beachcoma.

Norman immediately ordered a Jack Daniels—and then made it two. It was the first visit to the 'Coma for the models. They took the last three stools at the bar while the rest of the patrons sullenly returned to their seats.

Starr pulled out his cell phone and tried Cook's number. But he got only the rapid busy signal again, no service. They were on their own out here.

And they needed some assistance.

"We could use a few more bodies, and a couple more vehicles, to help us cover the island quicker," Starr told the patrons, thinking the Escalades might still get around in the bad weather. "Anyone want to go? Maybe find out what's going on?"

No one moved. No one even looked at him.

"Might be just an hour or so," he added. "Not too long …

Still nothing . . .

Starr wasn't that surprised. If you're wealthy enough, spending Christmas in your island mansion was not a bad way to go. And if there was a snowstorm on Christmas

Eve, then you've got fodder for boozy stories to tell for years to come.

But a double blizzard? A once-in-a-millennium two-punch bomb cyclone? Mysterious explosions? No power?

It was time to head for Boca.

But then, suddenly, the bartender tore off his apron, retrieved a .45 automatic from under the bar, grabbed his parka and joined Starr's party near the door. He was Jerry. A very big guy.

"They're all hedge fund assholes," he whispered to Starr. "Big mouths, but no guts."

Their brief respite over, the team retrieved their weapons and put their foul weather gear back on—all except Coward who'd meekly volunteered to stay at the bar and watch over the models and the patrons. Jerry would have to do his best to squeeze into Coward's small piece of the plow's back seat.

Starr pulled the bar's door open and the blizzard blew in. He fought to keep it open as the team members put their shoulders to the wind and went out one at a time.

Once they'd gone, Starr glanced back at the patrons. The team had to find the DIY gun—or guns—but now they also had to protect these people. And judging from the nonresponse just now, that might be a chore.

"We'll be back in an hour," he told Coward. "If all goes well."

Starr put up his parka hood and pushed his way out into the storm.

Jackson was right in front of him. As they made their way to the snowplow, they passed the half dozen luxury cars in the parking lot. Five were now buried by drifts. Only the sun-bright Banana Lambo was visible, but it was being so fiercely pummeled by the superstorm's high winds, it looked like it was going to blow away.

"Only an idiot would have a car like that out here in the winter," Jackson yelled over the gale to Starr.

Jackson climbed into the plow's cab and back behind the wheel. Starr made sure everyone else was onboard and then climbed in himself. He squeezed in next to Norman, already two Jack Daniels into the game. He was about to say something to the old guy when he saw that his mouth had fallen wide open and his eyes seemed to be coming out of their sockets.

He was pointing to something over Starr's shoulder.

Starr's antennas went up. He saw it an instant before he saw it for real.

Rumbling down Center Street, blowing a lot of smoke and sounding like a truck without a muffler, was a snow covered, ice encrusted M1 Abrams battle tank.

Chapter Eleven

It was a monster.

Sixty-five tons of gun, armor, tracks and treads. It was throwing up massive plumes of snow behind it as it approached, black smoke pouring from its backend, its gigantic 120mm cannon pointed right at the plow. They heard it shift gears, and suddenly it was coming at them even faster.

But . . . this didn't make sense. The Abrams was the U.S. military's main battle tank; America's big rolling gun, maybe the best tank in the world. What the hell was one doing out here?

Norman was the first to shoot at it. He yelled: "I got this—I was in Korea!" then jumped from the cab, brought his shotgun up to his waist and began blasting away. The rest of the team fell out behind him and started shooting at the behemoth too. In a very irrational moment, it seemed like the only rational thing to do.

Starr was right in the middle of it, firing his Glock just as fast as he could pull the trigger. Sparks were flying everywhere; the noise was tremendous. The street was enveloped by an earsplitting light show, so many guns were going off at once.

But it did no good. Everything they fired at the tank pinged off its armor plating, creating more sparks, more noise, but little else. Not only did their fusillade not slow down the tank, its driver did another gear shift and now it was coming at them even faster.

Deputy Andy was nearest to the snowplow. He jumped in the cab, threw the truck in gear and stomped on the gas. The plow lurched forward about ten feet before the engine stalled. But it was enough to avoid getting hit by the tank.

The rest of them dove for cover. The ground shook like in an earthquake as the M1 thundered by. In its wake, a thick smell of gasoline and smothering belches of smoke. It screeched to a stop at the end of Center Street, fifteen feet from the burning ferry dock. There was a small park here, a couple benches and an old flagpole ready to snap in the wind.

The tank started moving again, but in a herky-jerky fashion. It seemed to be trying to get closer to the flagpole, while staying away from the burning pier. But it was impossible to do. It just couldn't avoid the blowing flames.

Then came a loud cough from the M-1's engine. The tank made an awkward, disjointed, right hand turn and, hidden by another burst of dirty exhaust, disappeared back into the storm.

All this happened in about ten seconds.

"What the fuck was that?" Jerry the bartender shouted over the howling wind.

Even Jackson, the older vet, was shaken. "Terrorists? With a tank? Out here?" he yelled.

"I don't give a crap who it is," Deputy Andy bellowed above them all. "If they wanted to scare the shit out of me, mission accomplished."

All the while Starr was trying to push a new clip into his Glock. Everyone was reloading. They looked at him, as if to say: What should we do?

But Starr didn't have to wait for the question.

He yelled into the gale: "We've got to go after it!"

Chapter Twelve

The team scrambled back into the snowplow.

Jackson went behind the wheel again; Starr took the passenger side, up front. They lowered the plow blades and took off down Center Street. Going right at the flagpole, they skidded onto a bumpy, icy, barely paved road even narrower than the one they took up from the boat ramp.

But incredibly they could see the tank's exhaust flare through the snow. That's how hot its engine was running. But it was way out in front of them, moving towards the nature preserve on the north end of the island. Fraught with sand dunes and thickets of plumbush trees, if the M-1 reached the sanctuary, there would be plenty of places for it to hide.

So Jackson began laying on the gas and in seconds the big plow was going almost 50mph, its huge blades tossing aside immense amounts of snow. They soon entered the nature preserve—its gate had been knocked down and crushed. The road narrowed even further here and there were ditches on both sides. Dense and entwined plumbush trees were blowing crazily over their heads. Yet the tank was still in sight and they were gaining on it.

But then the plow ran head-on into a massive gust of snow, so powerful it knocked the big truck sideways. Suddenly they were driving blind. Jackson stood on the brakes, jostling everyone on board. They skidded to a stop just inches before a ditch.

It took a long explicative-laced minute before the gust passed. When they could see again, the tank was gone.

Now what?

Starr turned on the truck's powerful searchlight. It illuminated both the snow and the tracks the tank had left behind.

"Follow the yellow brick road," Jackson yelled. He pushed the accelerator back to the floor and they were soon speeding along again.

"I can't wait to find out what this son of a bitch is doing out here . . ." Norman declared to the approval of the others.

But as one part of Starr's brain concentrated on the best way to keep the searchlight directed on the tank's tracks—about ten feet in front of the big V-blade seemed to work the best—another part began thinking about something else.

Priorities . . .

Keep them straight.

Actually, what the Abrams was doing out here was something to be answered later. The goal now was to stop it from firing at anyone again.

Just like shooting at it, chasing the tank seemed like the thing to do at the time. But what if they caught it? Their rifles and pistols were useless against its armor. They were never going to stop it with bullets alone. And it could take them out with one shot. Destroying the snowplow would be a lot easier than trying to sink the ferry.

They had three options: knock out the tank's engine, disable its drive sprockets somehow, or . . . kill whoever was inside causing all this mayhem. That would be the quickest way to solve the problem, but also the most distasteful.

Suddenly Jackson brought the plow to another noisy stop.

They'd reached an intersection that was partially shielded from the storm by another canopy of plumbush trees. Starr trained the light on the crossroads to reveal the tank's tread pattern had changed. To their right the tracks went up a wide, sandy path heading east towards the ocean. But there was another set that continued straight down the bumpy dirt road towards the northern tip of the island.

But not a few feet up from that, they could see a *third* set of tracks that went left, across a field of frozen saw-grass and over a nearby dune.

"There's more than one of them?" Jerry asked.

"No, they're the same tracks," Jackson said. "Just made at different times."

Starr added soberly: "It doesn't have to stick to the roads like we do. Sand dunes, the beach. The marshes. These thickets. It's a tank. It can go anywhere it wants—and we can't."

They were all quiet for a few moments. The wind kept howling, and they couldn't see more than a few inches outside the window, the snow was blowing so heavily.

They were very much alone out here, in the middle of nowhere, engine roaring, searchlight ablaze.

The perfect place for an ambush. And they were a big target.

Jackson felt it too.

Starr asked him: "When is discretion the better part of valor?"

But Jackson was already starting to turn around.

"When you don't have to tell me twice," he said.

Chapter Thirteen

They returned to the Beachcoma to find the patrons had not moved from their seats.

The models had taken a table in the corner by themselves. Coward reported the girls had quickly become bored of the money heads and their significant others non-stop griping.

While Jackson, Norman and Deputy Jim agreed to take the first watch outside, Deputy Andy explained the situation to the people in the bar. The patrons were alarmed, but at a loss as to what they could do.

On hearing the news, though, Tina, Tami and Trish poured three large cups of coffee, and brought them to the men outside. They made it clear they were ready to pitch in.

Starr never stopped trying to raise Cookie. Sitting at the other end of the bar, drinking a quick coffee, he kept redialing the chief's number obsessively, getting nothing but busy signals in return. After a couple dozen tries, he did little more than wear down his battery. Finally he turned the phone off, but only to save the last of his juice.

It made it all even more maddening to him, though. A very bizarre thing was happening not a mile away from Old Seabury and there was no way Starr could raise the alarm. The blizzard was still blowing at full fury. There was a freaking tank on the loose out there somewhere. And he was stuck in a bar babysitting a bunch of One Percent malcontents.

What a way to spend Christmas Eve.

But then . . . very suddenly . . . his senses began buzzing again. At last, some help was coming from the great beyond.

He closed his eyes and thought: *Here we go again . . .*

On Starr's short list of STPA2 abilities was something the Navy shrinks dubbed VGM, for video-graphic memory.

Similar to an eidetic or photographic memory, Starr could recall sequences of certain events in great detail, almost as if he was watching a video. He could wind forward and back. He could freeze frame. He could zoom in on things he hadn't seen before. Like most of his pre-cog shrinkage, VGM tended to come in bursts. He had to use it when he could.

He rewound back to when the tank first appeared. No question, it was an M1 Abrams. They were unmistakable. But looking at it a second time, there were a few peculiar things about it. True, it was carrying a monstrous 120mm main gun, its standard armament. But these beasts also carried two 30-mm machine guns along with a 50-caliber muthafucker on the turret. Yet this tank had none of these weapons.

Nor were there any antennas. Or infrared sights. It was also blowing so much smoke, its gas turbine engine was probably not running up to peak.

Starr ran another scene back and forth. It showed how the tank acted once it went by them while they were reloading. It had lingered for those few moments near the burning ferry dock next to the flagpole, almost as if deciding what to do. Only when it found it could not get past the dock fire did it turn right and head down the bumpy icy road leading to the nature preserve.

Starr saw something else he hadn't noticed before. Before the tank vanished into the storm, its turret had turned right first and then, only after a few seconds passed, did the tracks begin to move, turning the rest of the tank as well.

It was a strange, awkward maneuver.

Why didn't everything turn at the same time?

Jerry the bartender refilled Starr's coffee cup.

"I'm not so sure about this being a terrorist thing," he said in a hushed voice. "I mean, any chance that some wealthy guy out here might have *bought* this thing? Like from Army Surplus?'

Starr shrugged. "They go for at least fifteen million new."

Jerry laughed. "That's pocket change to some of these d-bags."

Starr dumped a handful of sugar packets into his coffee, stirred it briskly and then took a swig. "No matter who's driving it, though—crazy rich guy or terrorist—they know we're all in here."

"You think it will come back?"

"We have to assume it will," Starr said, retrieving his parka, ready to battle the storm again. "We've got to be prepared for that."

As he was saying this, Starr's gaze fell on a bottle of scotch on the shelf nearby. Johnnie Walker Blue. Expensive stuff, flowing like water back at the Kleinpeter-Morosi household he was sure.

Jerry saw him staring at the bottle, opened it and poured some into Starr's coffee.

"It'll make staying awake more fun," he said.

Starr thanked him and took a sip of the laced coffee. It tasted terrible—great scotch on top of packet sugar. But he downed it in four gulps.

He began to put on his parka, but stopped for a moment and slumped against the bar, cold, wet and tired.

He wondered what Angel was doing at that moment.

Chapter Fourteen

Boston

Powered by its own generator, the Christmas party at the Kleinpeter-Morosi brownstone was elegant and entertaining as usual. Great food. Great booze. Great conversation.

But Angel was not enjoying herself.

She was worried about Starr. This time, more than usual.

It took a couple hours, but she'd finally been able to gracefully disappear from the gathering. Climbing to the top floor of her parent's mansion, she sat next to the large picture window. It looked out on Boston Harbor and the ocean beyond.

She'd spent a long time, gazing out at the storm. And she'd imagined a few times that, just for a moment, she could see through all the blowing snow, down along the southern coastline where the lights of tiny Old Seabury and some of Cape Cod were visible on clear nights.

Chris was out there, somewhere. Doing things other people couldn't conceive of. And she knew that he was an expert in taking care of himself.

But now, not an hour into Christmas Day, she couldn't shake the feeling that he needed her help.

She finally went downstairs, quietly grabbed her mother's parka and snow boots—and the keys to her Prius.

But her father caught her at the front door, whiskey tumbler in hand.

"You're going out in this weather?" he asked her.

"Just for a little while," she replied softly.

"Is it Chris?" her dad asked. "Is he OK?"

She smiled. Her father *always* knew.

"I'm sure he is," she said. "But I've *got* to make sure . . ."

He smiled back. Then he took the Prius keys from her—and handed her the FOB to his Range Rover instead.

"It rides better in the snow," he said with a wink.

Chief Cook was also cold, wet and exhausted.

He was sitting in his patrol car, parked back on Water Street, after just having evacuated the last family from Old Seabury's east side. Just about the entire town was now jammed into the old fallout shelter at the Vo-tech regional high.

He was the only one here now . . . sitting alone in his own little ghost town.

What the hell is going to happen next? he wondered.

A moment later he saw two faint beams approaching in the storm. Headlights, moving very fast.

This was odd. There was a driving ban in effect and only emergency vehicles were allowed on the roads. Yet he saw no flashing lights, could hear no siren.

Through the snow came a large SUV-type vehicle, driving at top speed. The driver saw his police car and came to a skidding stop. They got out wearing what looked to be an oversized parka and ran over to his cruiser.

Cook lowered his window halfway. "Do you need help?" he yelled into the blowing snow.

The driver came up close and pulled down the parka's hood. At that moment Cook realized he was looking at the most beautiful woman he'd ever seen.

"Hi—do you know Chris Starr?" she asked him.

Her voice was so sweet, Cook fumbled for a reply; he was simply dazzled by her.

Then he put it together.

Finally he said: "You must be Angel . . ."

They spent the next ten minutes in his police car, drinking two cappuccinos that Angel had somehow managed to buy along the way.

Cook briefed her on the last few hours in Old Seabury, from the first building to get blown up to when Starr and the rescue party left on the ferry.

"What about the Feds?" she asked. "State police? Anybody?"

"No way to get a message out," Cookie told her. "Though we keep trying. The only cell tower in town blew over and all the land lines are out too. No internet, no mobile service."

Angel looked across the bay and could just barely see the barrier island in the distance, and then only through intermittent openings in the gales of snow.

"So, we don't know what's happening out there then?" she asked.

Cook shook his head. "Sorry, we don't."

Chapter Fifteen

It took Starr and the team a half hour to erect a barricade across Center Street.

Stretching from the 'Coma's bar entrance to the boarded-up candle shop on the opposite side, they built it using old wooden pallets found in the 'Coma's basement. Much of the wood was soaked with tar which helped hold the barrier together. The team then reinforced the wall with electrical wire, rope and duct tape. It now stood eight feet high and was about 20 feet long.

They knew the barricade, just like their gunfire, would not stop the M-1 on its own. But it might slow it down—and that's what they wanted.

Killing the beast, they'd decided, could come down to one lucky bullet round. The Abrams was powered by gasoline; its fuel compartment was just behind the turret. If the team could get the monster to falter just a bit, and they fired at it from behind, they might be able to hit its gas tank.

But they had a second trick up their sleeves. They'd also found a dozen lengths of six-foot steel pipe in the 'Coma's basement. What would happen if they jammed a few of them into the tank's sprockets? Would it break the track and grind the tank to a halt?

They knew both options were long shots.

But they had to try.

It was now 1:00 a.m.

The wind had picked up, the snow became even heavier. Between the roar of the storm and the sound of waves crashing on the beach nearby, conversation was impossible. The team had to communicate by hand signals. And while the three models continued to brave the elements to keep the team warm with coffee, the bar patrons chose to simply watch it all from the inside, huddled around the 'Coma's candlelit windows, pausing only to get more drinks.

As soon as the barrier was complete, the candles in the 'Coma were doused and the models and the patrons were herded inside the bar's beer cooler, the safest place in the house.

Starr was manning the center of the barricade, his Glock ready, three ammo clips in reserve. Norman was to his right with Coward anchoring their flank. To the left stood Jerry the bartender and Deputy Jim. Jackson and Deputy Andy were about twenty feet behind them, waiting next to the pile of pipes.

A deathly calm fell over Center Street; the tension was thick in the air. Ears-up, heads turning in all directions, fighting off the snow and wind, the team tried to detect any indication that the tank was coming—and from which direction.

Twenty anxious minutes into this, Starr felt a tug on his sleeve. It was the younger vet, Joel Coward. He was shaking from both the cold and his nerves.

"I've got a confession," he told Starr, his voice wavering. "I was in the Army, but I was a tech, you know? I never saw any action; I never even left the United States."

"So?" Starr asked him.

Coward paused and then said: "So . . . I'm no hero."

Starr almost laughed. "Well, you're here, aren't you?"

They heard the tank a moment later.

Chapter Sixteen

It came out of the blinding, swirling snow from the same direction, trailing the same wake of oily black smoke.

The team opened up on it immediately—but as planned, with only one barrage. Firing from behind the barrier, they made a lot of noise, their gun flashes lighting up the ferociously windy night, once again sparks flying everywhere. But as before, everything they fired just bounced off the tank.

The monster was moving faster this time—and it was coming right at them, now just 100 feet away. The team reloaded, but held their fire.

But then the M-1 abruptly stopped. Its turret began to move.

Luckily Starr saw it two seconds before it happened.

He yelled: "Everyone down!"

The tank's big gun fired.

The 120mm high-explosive round screamed over the barrier, trailing a massive stream of bright orange flame behind it. It hit what was left of the burning ferry dock, blowing it into a million burning splinters and finally dousing the fire.

But the heat from the big gun's blast was so intense, the barricade's tar covered pallets instantly burst into flame, throwing the team back on its heels.

Starr's left sleeve caught fire; he put it out with a handful of snow. Norman's wool cap also ignited, but Starr put that out the same way. All of the team members were frantically staunching flames on themselves.

The M1 was lost inside the cloud of smoke and dust caused by the big gun's firing. But when the smoke blew away, the team was surprised to see through the barricade's flames that the creature hadn't moved. Exhaust was belching from its back end and once again, the smell of gasoline was thick in the air. But the M1 remained absolutely still.

Twenty seconds went by.

Thirty . . . .

Starr's instincts began buzzing; he knew what was going on. Whoever was in command of the tank was trying to make up their mind about what to do next.

Unusual . . . especially in a combat situation when five seconds seems like an eternity.

The team had hoped the tank would crash through the barrier—on fire or not—and slow down enough for them to push the pipes into the sprockets and deliver the fusillade to its rear end, hoping the Cosmos helped them hit the fuel supply. But in this frozen moment, both seemed like extremely long shots.

Finally, the tank's gears shifted and its engine revved up. The team tensed. The monster started moving again.

It began heading right for the flaming barrier, at full speed, just as they wanted. But about 50 feet from the barricade, the tank suddenly swerved right—and crashed into the Beachcoma instead.

This was the loudest noise of all, a gigantic, deafening *crunch!* Pieces of the building flew off in all directions, bringing down a rain of glass and concrete chips on top of the already singed team.

The tank went straight through the bar, through the waiting area and burst out near the main entrance. It took a few seconds to flatten one of the snow covered Beemers in the parking lot, but then it kept right on going, trailing its own little storm of black smoke.

With amazing courage, Jackson and Deputy Andy started running alongside it, each shoving a steel pipe into its sprockets. They might have slowed the tank, but not by much and not for very long. There were lots of sparks and crackling noises, but the tracks quickly demolished the pipes, sending pieces of jagged steel flying around as well.

Jackson and Andy cleared the area and the team delivered their fusillade to the rear of the tank. But they were firing into a 90-mile gale of blinding snow and hoping for the luckiest of shots even in the best of conditions. The barrage was intense, and whether they hit the Abrams or not, its fuel tank was unaffected.

In a case of déjà vu, the Abrams reached the end of the street, and stopped close to the flagpole, being careful to avoid the last smoldering parts of the pier nearby.

But then the tank slowly turned towards the mainland, adjusted its turret slightly and—*blam!* Another explosion of fire and smoke flew out of its gun. The team could see the trail of the sizzling tank shell as it disappeared into the storm, heading for Old Seabury.

The recoil from the blast shook the street under their feet again. And once more, the Abrams was enveloped in a cloud of snow and smoke.

They heard a flurry of gear shifting, saw the turret point forward again, with the rest of the tank slowly following suit. One more grind of the gears and it disappeared down the same bumpy road leading to the nature preserve.

In all, the strange battle had lasted just twenty seconds.

Jackson was quickly at Starr's side.

"Are we going to chase it again?" he asked, out of breath.

But Starr just shook his head. Something *very* unusual was happening here.

"Not this time," he said.

Chapter Seventeen

One minute before

Back in Old Seabury, Angel stood near the wreckage of the Peabody mansion, not believing her eyes.

There was no rubble; that might have been the strangest thing. Everything had been pulverized, blown to bits. Nothing was left.

"Chris thought it was an artillery shell of some kind," Chief Cook said.

He was standing beside her; both were being battered by the storm. She'd asked to see the scene of the bombing, and he'd complied.

"Did he taste the snow?" she asked.

Cook nodded. "He did."

"I know it's gross—but when he does that, he's usually right."

They headed back to the cruiser where a thermos of regular old coffee was waiting.

Before she climbed in, though, Angel looked out towards the island, trying again to spot it between the gusts of snow.

That's when she saw a bright light burning its way through the storm.

Coming right at them . . .

Her first thought was: *fireworks?*

Somehow, Cook knocked her to the ground as the shell went over their heads; they wound up in a tangle in a snowbank. It hit a second later—not on the empty space that used to be the Peabody house—but on a similarly ornate McMansion three blocks away on Lanesville Road.

The explosion rocked the waterfront. A massive cloud of orange flame shot up into the storm.

Cook scrambled to his feet, helped Angel up and dove into his cruiser. She jumped in with him. They were off in a second.

It took Cook less than a minute to reach Lanesville Road, driving like a madman through the raging snow.

They arrived to find another scene of complete destruction. This house, similar in size to the Peabody manse, had also been utterly demolished. There were a few fires burning here and there, but again, there was really nothing left to burn.

Cook couldn't believe it. "We just evacuated this area, not ten minutes before you arrived!"

"And you saw it this time," Angel told him. "Something coming from the island did this."

Cook took the next minute trying to get his cruiser's radio to work, but with no luck. Who was he going to call anyway? His entire force was tied up with getting the last of the civilians into the Vo-tech fallout shelter. The town's tiny fire department was up there helping as well and the State Police were still a no-show.

The chief shook his head wearily.

"This is like a bad dream," he confessed to Angel. "And I want to wake up. I mean, is someone out there trying to blow up our little town one house at a time? And are those poor guys out there trying to stop it? In this storm? I'm thinking now I shouldn't have let them go."

Angel put her hand on his.

"Chris would have gone anyway," she told him—and he knew she was right.

"I just wish we could talk to them out there," Cook said, finally throwing the radio mic onto the dashboard in despair. "Learn what the situation is. But there's literally no way to do it."

Angel bit her lip. She squeezed his hand tighter.

"Chief—what I'm about to show you, you can never discuss with anyone," she said. "It's a matter of national security."

Before he could reply, she reached into her Louie Vuitton bag and came out with what looked like an old and highly mistreated kid's walkie-talkie.

"*Very* top secret," she whispered.

She and Starr called it the tomato can.

And it *did* look like a toy, circa 1960 or so. Plastic cracked, a thin veneer of black paint flaking off, its screen scratched and scraped.

But when you turned it on, a second hidden screen lit up like the dash of a new Corvette. Deploy the little dish antenna and you were in business.

It was a satellite phone. It could work in any weather, just about anywhere on Earth. Starr had received a pair when he first started working for NILE. He gave one to Angel under the strict condition she used it only in emergencies. Truth was, she used it to call him all the time.

"You can talk to anyone in the world on this thing," she told Cook.

"Even in super blizzards?" he asked, still amazed at the device's bizarre disguise.

"We'll see," she replied.

She punched in Starr's special code—it was 21 numbers long. Then she entered a default code, essentially giving her access to the U.S. Navy's top secret sat phone network. And then his cell phone number.

His phone began to ring.

And ring.

And ring.

Chapter Eighteen

Half the Beachcoma had been destroyed.

The remains of crushed yellow cement blocks were everywhere. Pipes were leaking and steaming and sparking. Broken bottles and silverware were scattered in the snowbanks, glistening in the flames. Thick smoke was rising from the rubble. This is what happens when a 65-ton tank runs through your bar.

The patrons and the models had escaped harm by staying inside the bar's cooler, but it had been a frightening few seconds. The tank came within 20 feet of flattening them too.

Now everyone was gathered in the 'Coma's kitchen, located right behind the dining room. The electricity had gone out on the island long ago, but the kitchen's emergency generator was still working. Though dim, the lights were lit and the ovens still worked too. So it was warm.

The team was exhausted though. While the patrons liberated some cooking wine and started bitching about the flattened BMW, Starr and the others gathered in the opposite corner and talked quietly amongst themselves.

"Eventually that thing's going to come back and this time it's going to put a shell into the rest of this place," Deputy Jim said wearily.

Norman agreed. "Or just run us over."

"Maybe it's time to get out of here," Andy said.

"But how?" Jackson wanted to know. "We can't fit everyone into the snowplow. Even if we all stayed behind, the rest of them still couldn't do it. And where would they go?"

But Starr was just shaking his head. "I think we're safe," he said. "I don't think the tank will try to hurt us."

The others were surprised to hear this.

He explained: "Since we landed on this island, it's had two perfect opportunities to kill us already—and it didn't. It seems more interested on getting right next to that flagpole, to fire on Old Seabury."

"It's probably a positional point," Jackson said. "A place where a gunner knows, if I shoot it from here, there's a good chance it's going to hit where I want it to hit, over there. Perfect for preset targets. It's all in the triangulation."

"Freaking trigonometry," Jerry said.

"But there's something else," Starr went on. "Remember the ferry dock had been burning? Then the tank shot at it and that was the end of the fire—I think it came back over here just to put out that fire. And when our barricade went up in flames, it went through the bar instead. And when it stopped at the end of the street and finally fired its gun, it was very careful not to get anywhere near anything still burning."

"And all I can smell out there is gasoline," Coward added.

Starr nodded. "The only thing it's done consistently is stay away from fire. And that stink in the air? The hell with the fuel tank. I think this thing has been leaking gas the whole time . . ."

"That must be it," Jackson said after a few seconds. "It's afraid of fire . . ."

"Just like Frankenstein," Norman said.

As the other team members went back outside to rebuild the barricade, Starr and Jerry returned to the 'Coma's cellar.

The bar upstairs had been demolished and every liquor bottle smashed. But down here, most everything was still intact. Jerry led him to a small storage room.

"This is where those humps upstairs keep all their private stock," he said, revealing a cold, dark space filled with all kinds of high-end whiskey.

Starr recognized many of the names: Glenlivet Gold, MacGregor's Prime Cask, Jameson's Premier Stock.

"How much is all this worth?" he asked.

"Twenty grand at least," Jerry replied. "But I guarantee it will burn just as good as the cheap stuff."

They put together a case of the best liquor they could find and carried it up to the kitchen.

While the patrons stayed down near the ovens, Starr and Jerry took over a sink at the back. They emptied all the 'Coma's sugar shakers into a 15-gallon plastic jug from the kitchen's water cooler. Next came a box of heavy duty dishwashing detergent. Then every match and cigarette lighter they could find in the place. On top they poured nine thousand dollars' worth of highly combustible single malt whiskey.

Jerry shook the jug until the contents became a white, slushy mixture.

All this had taken five minutes tops.

When they were done, they'd made 15-gallons of very sticky, homemade napalm.

Chapter Nineteen

They set a trap.

Part one was to put the patrons back in the beer cooler. Part two was to put street the barrier back together again, fortified with cement blocks from the wreckage of the 'Coma's bar. The wall turned out sturdier and taller than before, but no one was hiding behind it this time.

Instead the team pushed the five remaining sports cars, including the million-dollar Banana Lambo, out into the snowy street and put them on the other side of the blockade.

The team's mantra was unchanged: they didn't have to stop the tank; they just had to slow it down. And of all the impediments the M1 had faced so far, including running through the 'Coma, crushing the first BMW took the longest—a mere pause at just three or four seconds.

But that might mean crushing five cars could take up to fifteen seconds or more.

And maybe that's all they needed.

Part three of the plan involved restricting the tank's movement.

If they were right, the tank crew was being overly cautious when it came to getting near any flames. So the team set up two huge bonfires at the end of Center Street—one blocking the bumpy road to the nature preserve, the other cutting off the access road they'd taken up from the boat ramp. They also built bonfires next to the candle shop and the remains of the 'Coma bar.

If the monster wanted to get to the flagpole, if it needed to be beside its positional point, then it would have to come down Center Street, just as it had twice before.

And if it was afraid of fire, it would have to go straight through their reconstituted barrier. There was no other way.

Jackson, Norman and Deputy Andy took up stations on the left side of the street, behind the fire near the candle shop. Deputy Jim, Coward and Jerry took the right side near the wrecked bar. Starr was farther down the street, near the Banana Lambo. Everyone was carrying two Molotov cocktails made from the DIY napalm. A line of homemade torches burned nearby; stuck in a huge snowbank, tended by the three models.

A half hour went by—the team was beyond antsy. But then they heard it again. Just as before, almost on cue, it came out of the snow at the far end of Center

Street, near the boardwalk to the outer beach. It clanked its way into a right hand turn and then stopped, clearly assessing the situation.

The team used the torches to light the bonfires. Four mushroom clouds of orange smoke shot into the stormy skies. The air was heavy with exhaust and the stink of gasoline was starting to creep into the winds.

They heard the familiar sound of big gears shifting. Its engine barked once and the tank shot forward. M1s could hit almost 50mph and this time, the beast was displaying no hesitation.

It hit the barricade full force and with a mighty crash, launching many of the yellow cement blocks back into the air again. The first in line BMW took the brunt of it; it was crushed in an instant. The second car—a Benz 720—was flattened almost as quickly.

But then the tank came down on top of the other Benz, a classic 713—and suddenly, there was a problem. Its gun had impaled the car through its front windshield and right back to the rear seat, literally halting the tank in its tracks. The tank crew added power and lifted the gun barrel, but it picked up the skewered Benz as well. It was hanging off the long gun like some kind of dead animal.

A quick burst of power and a violent twist of the turret sent the stricken car flying into the candle shop, destroying them both. But now the tank found itself sitting squarely on top of the last Beemer, three feet off the ground, its treads unable to get any traction.

The crew gunned the engine mightily. A soot-filled cloud of exhaust penetrated the snowstorm—and blew away in an instant. Another rev of the engine, more exhaust and suddenly the stench of gasoline was everywhere. Engine running at full rpms, the tank pitched forward slightly—but then stopped dead. Its engine had stalled.

The team sprang into action.

Like wild ice covered mad men, they ran out of the storm and started plastering the tank with the homemade napalm.

The attack was surprisingly coordinated. All twelve bottle bombs hit the stalled tank at just about the same time. This created not one, but two huge explosions: the combined napalm assault and a second later, a massive flash of fire as the thick gasoline vapors in the air ignited. The floundering tank was immediately consumed by the flames. It had indeed been leaking gasoline—and that gas was now feeding the blaze started by the DIY napalm. A process of self-immolation had begun.

Stationed at the 'Coma's kitchen's entrance, the models, in full frenzy, delivered three more boxes of Molotov Cocktails to the team. They launched a second barrage at the struggling creature, adding more flames to what was already an inferno.

The M1's turret hatch flew open. Smoke came pouring out. The monster was on the ropes.

Starr shouted over the wind. "Remember—if they don't come out shooting, we'll take them prisoner!"

The team brought their weapons to bear on the top of the burning tank, waiting for the crew to finally emerge.

But then . . . incredibly . . . the M1's engine suddenly roared back to life. Streams of multicolored smoke came pouring out of the turret's hatch, but its tracks started moving again. Now rocking back and forth, and grinding up what was left of the last BMW, it landed back on the snowy ground once more.

The tank staggered forward, pancaked the million-dollar Lambo and kept on going. Rivulets of blue flame were dripping off its sides, leaving a wide trail of fire in its wake. It looked like it was melting—but it was still alive.

Starr didn't see this coming. That was the problem.

Chasing it didn't work. Attacking its sprockets didn't work. Setting it on fire didn't work.

What was left?

He was suddenly running down the street, chasing the tank on foot.

Screw this, he thought.

Time for option four.

The M1 had roared to the end of Center Street and stopped next to the flagpole once again. It was still on fire, and was emitting not just a lot of smoke, but some unsettling electrical noises as well. But incredibly it was still able to operate.

Starr was running as fast as he could in the blizzard and in the heavy parka. The rest of the team was right behind him. He heard someone yell: "Watch out—it's going to fire again!"

Then . . . several things happened at once. There was a loud bang and smoke started absolutely pouring out of the tank's open hatch. The turret itself had started to move, but as it was doing so, its big gun fired—or mis-fired. The sound of the blast shook the island—but the shell sizzled its way through the blowing snow for only a couple hundred yards before falling into the bay. It did not explode. An obvious malfunction, the M1 suddenly revved itself up and started moving again.

That's when Starr jumped on its back.

And a moment after that, Jerry the bartender jumped on too.

The rest of the team had arrived at the end of the street by now. The last they saw of Starr and Jerry, they were climbing up the back of the burning tank just as it was dodging the nearby bonfire.

Then, with another roar of its engine, it disappeared into the raging snow once again.

Chapter Twenty

Angel and Starr lived a crazy life; she was used to all sorts of weirdness. But Old Seabury was in such a bizarre state, it was taking a little time to sink in.

The tiny postcard town was being shelled by some kind of weapon on the island across the bay, in a mega-blizzard, and there was nothing anyone could do about it—except her *uber*-boyfriend, who was presently on that island.

This was one for the books.

She was worried about him. She had to talk to him and know he was all right. But—she also had to tell him what had been happening on this side of the water, in Old Seabury itself.

The town had been evacuated, but another huge home had been destroyed—she'd seen it herself. And neither the state police nor the Feds had reached the town yet.

Even more bizarre: Cook was beginning to think the two McMansions were not random targets . . .

But every time Angel called Starr on the tomato can, she heard nothing but the rapid-fire busy signal, causing her heart to sink a little lower. She tried over and over, at least twenty times, before slamming it *s*hut.

"It's that piece of crap phone of his," Cook consoled her. "He shut it off to save power. That's all . . ."

"I hope so," she replied.

But it *was* frustrating. "How can we tell him to turn on his phone when his phone is turned off?" she sighed. "It's impossible."

Cook thought a moment and then said: "Maybe not . . ."

Chapter Twenty-One

The M1 was moving so fast, it was completely leaving the snowy ground at times, only to crash back down twice as hard again.

Luckily Starr and Jerry had grabbed onto a metal grate attached to the back of the tank's turret. The M1's crew could not have known they were here, as one sweep of the turret would have tossed them off the back.

But still, what they were doing was nuts.

The turret hatch was still wide open. Starr could hear it clanging away every time they went over a bump. The tank's engine was getting louder by the second, and parts of its armored skin were still on fire. Everything else was covered with gasoline, hydraulic fluid, transmission fluid and plain old motor oil.

All this was slippery making it difficult to hold on. And though he and Jerry couldn't converse over the racket of the engine, they both knew what Starr was going to do and that he better do it quickly.

Starr wasn't in love with what had to happen next. It wasn't like he'd never been in this position before, but the tank crew had chosen not to shoot at them on two occasions. Now, unfortunately, Starr wasn't able to return the favor.

His plan was to climb to the turret and fire an entire clip from the Glock into the open hatchway. It was tight quarters below, all of it steel and electronics. Bullets tended to split and ricochet in such circumstances, bad news for anyone inside.

And if that didn't do the trick, Jerry was right behind him, with his .45 automatic.

Starr started to climb up onto the turret. They were already quite a distance down the bumpy, icy road. If he didn't move fast, no matter what the outcome, they'd be stranded out here, a long walk from any kind of warmth or shelter—in the middle of the still raging double bombogenesis.

He grabbed onto a handle on top of the turret and pulled himself up. He slipped the safety off on his Glock.

But then he felt Jerry hitting him on the leg. The bartender was pointing towards Old Seabury. A large red light had appeared over the water. It was so bright they could see it clearly through the blowing snow.

This was *very* strange. The light was so intense they would have noticed it before.

The M1 hit an especially big bump and left the ground again. Starr and Jerry had only an instant to brace themselves before the tank slammed back down to the icy road once more.

It was violent and painful jolt. But they hardly felt it. They were still mesmerized by the bright red light.

"What the hell is that?" Jerry shouted over the racket. "Where's it coming from?"

Suddenly the light started blinking—and Starr knew instantly it was blinking in code.

Morse Code.

He began reading it. *Turn . . . on . . . flip.*

"Damn," he yelled into the wind.

Hanging on with one arm, he reached into his cargo pants and pulled out his old flip phone.

Jerry looked at him like he'd gone mad. Then the bartender started pointing frantically at something in front of them.

Starr flipped open the phone and hit the power button. It started ringing immediately.

He answered to hear the sweetest sound he could ever imagine.

It was Angel.

But at the very same moment, he saw something two seconds in his future. A low overhanging plumbush branch was coming his way.

He heard her say: "Chris?"

He said: "Angel?"

And then . . . *wham!*

Chapter Twenty-Two

Starr remembered a brief moment when he was airborne, tumbling in the blowing winds, his feet above him one instant, below him the next.

Then he slammed down into a snowbank. The superstorm's precipitation was not the light and fluffy kind; still it broke his fall and prevented serious injury. But he was at least three feet into the drift and now the snow was under his jacket, under his shirt, in his pants and boots.

He didn't care, though. He clawed his way out of the drift, fell onto the road—and immediately hit redial on the flipper.

The phone rang once—and then she answered.

Angel . . . .

"I'm here!" he shouted into the phone. "Are you okay?"

"I am now," he heard her say.

"Where the hell are you? In a UFO?"

"You said never to joke about that," she replied. "And no—we're in the Old Seabury lighthouse. We've been flashing the big light hoping you'd see us. Cookie is here and everything is OK at the moment. But—we don't know how long this connection will last. So, just listen . . ."

Then, Angel being Angel, she told him everything all at once by speaking as fast as she could.

She drove to Old Seabury on a hunch. She ran into Chief Cook. She saw the wreck of the first mansion and witnessed a second mansion getting hit just minutes ago.

Starr, in turn, told her everything that had happened on the island, quickly detailing their clashes with the tank. Between breaths Angel repeated every word to Cook. It sounded like complete madness—but she knew every word of it was true.

But she still had a very important piece of information for him.

The second house in the town that had been flattened may not have been a random target.

Angel went on: "The first house belonged to a high-priced attorney who is not the most popular guy in town. The second house belongs to a judge with whom this lawyer apparently does a lot of business. Both just beat a federal rap for colluding on raising clients' fees and conspiracy to commit insurance fraud. Cookie is sure there's a connection!"

But then suddenly, Starr's battery light began blinking.

Then the line went dead.

That's how Jerry found him. On the road, next to the snowbank, trying to call Angel back.

Chapter Twenty-Three

The rest of the team had jumped in the plow and had gone roaring down the icy, bumpy road, beginning a desperate search for Starr and Jerry.

Once more, it was a crowded cab. The four members of the original team plus Norman—along with Tami, Tina and Trish. Just as cold and wet and miserable as the rest of them, the three models insisted they go too.

Incredibly, after about 20 minutes of hard and fast plowing, the team came upon their wayward colleagues walking down the bumpy snow-covered road. The big plow pulled over and shined the searchlight down at the two men. Both were covered with wet, icy snow, head to boots. They looked like ghosts.

Their teammates hauled them up into the warm, overcrowded cab. There were hugs all round, including from the girls. In fact, the girls came close to kissing them both; Starr could tell. They squeezed him and Jerry in and the trio of models immediately snuggled up to them, to provide warmth. They did not complain.

"We were just starting to get worried," Jackson told them, the snowplow revving high in idle.

"Thanks for coming after us," Starr told them. There were now ten people squished into a cab built for six at the most. "Hope you're not making any more stops though."

He gave them the highlights of what had just transpired and what Angel had told him during their quick conversation. The models sighed wistfully on hearing Starr and his girlfriend had communicated in such an odd fashion as a blinking lighthouse.

"So romantic," Trish swooned.

But Jerry had even bigger tale to tell.

He'd not only witnessed the blinking light but also saw Starr go flying off the end of the tank—tumbling head over heels and disappearing into the winds of the blizzard.

"It happened so quick, before I could process it, I lost sight of him," Jerry said. "I was ready to jump off the back of the tank and go back and get him, but before I could, that bastard turned off the road—and into a long driveway hidden by those freaking plumbush trees. It led to this big old cottage. Its automatic door opened up and the tank headed right for the garage. I jumped off just as the door was coming down on me. I just ran like hell to get back in the storm so no one would see me. Then I came upon the lieutenant."

Jackson asked the question everyone wanted to know.

"What cottage is it?"

"That saucer-shaped thing off the road just before you get to the preserve," Jerry told them. "It's called the End of the World or something. That thing is hiding in there."

Chapter Twenty-Four

They had no trouble following the tank's tracks.

More snow had fallen so the tread impressions were fresh, plus the M1 was leaking a variety of hot, oily fluids. The plow slowly drove up to the bumpy road to cut-off, getting as close as they dared to the driveway. Jackson stopped behind an especially dense thicket of plumbush trees and they planned what would come next.

Many people on the island named their cottages. It was a tradition that went back to the good old days, when the names were clever, or at least not calculated to be whimsical.

This place was called The Very End of the World and it wasn't just saucer shaped—it was shaped like a *flying* saucer. Sitting atop a dune, surrounded by more dunes, it was two-circular stories with multiple porches, porthole style windows and a garage that looked like some kind of re-entry bay. Everything was covered with well-worn wooden shingles; its shutters flapping in the brutal wind.

The cottage screamed the 1960s. Located a mile north of the center, it had been vacant for years.

There was a widow's walk on the roof's peak with a look-out room just below it. The only illumination the crew could see was a single light burning inside this glass cupola.

"Someone told me the place had been rented a few years ago," Jerry said. "But I didn't think anyone ever moved in. We never saw anybody in town who said they were living out here."

"Maybe they didn't drink," Norman observed.

"Or maybe these guys just took over the place because they knew it was empty and that the storm was going to hit," Deputy Jim said. "But I'd still like to see how they managed to get a freaking tank out here. At the very least, those things make a lot of noise. They're hard to miss."

"Any guess how many guys are in the crew?" Coward asked Starr.

"I'm thinking now that there might not be a crew," Starr said, once more surprising the others. "Just the way it's been acting. I think it could be just one guy. One very ingenious and, I think, very angry guy."

"Why do you say that?" Deputy Jim asked.

Starr explained: "The first time we saw the tank, we surprised him as much as he surprised us. I think that's clear. A working tank crew would have fired on us. He just drove on through. The second time, he had to stop to fire that round at the boathouse—which could have just as easily gone right through us on its way. I think it was aimed over our heads intentionally."

"M1s can fire on the run—that's what makes them so special. But this one hasn't, so maybe it can't because there's only one guy involved, and he does all the driving and all the shooting. That means he has to stop, crawl out of the driver's position, climb up to the loader's position, take out a round, put it in the gun, then get into the gunner's seat, aim it and fire it.

"That's time intensive. Even if he has one in the chamber, it's still a lot of moving around. A crew could do it in maybe ten seconds. He takes a lot longer."

Starr studied the strange house through the blowing snow.

"And again, he chose not to kill us. That means there's a conscience working there. But it's not a warrior's conscience. Add to what Angel just told me about what's going on over on the mainland. That the houses it hit might have been targeted and what have we got?"

"Not a terrorist," Jackson said. "Not a typical one anyway."

Starr nodded. "Right—but he's definitely got a beef with some people on the mainland."

The team faced a grim task.

They had to end this for good. They couldn't let the big gun fire again and that meant destroying the old flying-saucer cottage and trying to kill whoever was inside it.

And it would not be a single-pistol operation—and nothing like what Starr had in mind before he got bounced off the tank. This would be a substantial attack, simply because they had the firepower.

It was the three models who'd suggested the team bring along their last case of Molotov Cocktails, just in case they were needed during the search for Jerry and Starr. They also retrieved a blow torch from the 'Coma's basement just in case the bottle bombs had to be lit in the raging snowstorm.

Both would come in handy.

*****

There were a dozen bottle bombs in all.

But as soon as the team members left the snowplow, with the girls agreeing to watch over the truck, they began to think a dozen firebombs might be overkill. The stink of gasoline was so thick around the huge circular cottage, even in the ferocious wind the men had to cover their faces to avoid breathing too much of it. And it only got stronger the closer they moved towards the house.

"A lit cigarette would level this place," Jackson told Starr as they slowly crept up the driveway. "We could get high from all these fumes."

"Yeah, lucky us," Starr replied gloomily.

He didn't feel any better about this than he did about the prospect of firing his Glock directly into the tank's compartment.

But some things just had to be done—right?

They formed a semi-circle on the west side of the house, not ten feet away from its multitude of bottom floor, porthole shaped windows. Once again, the storm provided all the cover they needed.

"Hope there are no kids in there!" Jerry whispered loudly.

"There aren't," Starr said. He just knew.

Deputy Andy had the blow torch out and fired up. Each man had two cocktails and each one was lit on the first try. On three, the team hurled their firebombs through the first floor porthole windows. Then they retreated as fast as they could back into the fiercely blowing snow.

Once again, all the bombs exploded at once. And once again, there were so many gas fumes in the area, there was another second, larger blast as the fog of flammable vapor suddenly ignited. By this time the team members had dove into the heavy drifts next to the driveway, protected by the heaps of snow.

They could hear more gasoline exploding inside the cottage along with lots of ammunition. The building was quickly engulfed in flames.

Face down in the snow, battered, frozen and bone-tired, Starr begged the Cosmos to end this miserable piece of business.

But . . . incredibly, in an explosion of wood and sparks, the tank burst out of the burning building's garage, roared down the driveway and went by them like a banshee.

It took a left out of the driveway, sped past the snow-plow and once again, disappeared into the stormy night.

"This is getting ridiculous now," Jackson cried, helping Starr out of the snowbank. "This thing is like a freaking cat. Nine lives."

But Starr was not completely disappointed. "We took away his base of operations," he said. "We destroyed what must have been his main source of fuel, ammo and who knows what else."

He looked at the snow on the driveway. The tank had left behind several thick trails of oily liquids. One was burned hydraulic fluid, the other was definitely gasoline.

Then he added: "Plus, this time, we know exactly where he's going . . ."

Chapter Twenty-Five

Once back in the snowplow, they followed the tank's tracks back down the bumpy road, through a cut off that went up to the ocean side and after a right hand turn, onto the beachside road that ran to the middle of the island. No surprise, they wound up back on Center Street.

But the tank was already there.

Looking down from the ocean side, past the half-flattened 'Coma, past the remains of their barricade and the trampled sports cars—there was the Abrams, smoking and wheezing, parked near the remains of the ferry dock and right next to the flagpole.

The positional point . . .

The creature was in even worse shape now. Smoke was pouring out of dozens of holes in its armor. Its engine was running erratically, as if it was trying to catch its breath. Its big gun was fully depressed, giving the impression of a warrior knight mortally wounded, his battle lance finally earthbound. The flagpole, completely bent over by the wind by now, looked like it had its arm around the tank's shoulder. The Abrams wasn't dead, but finally, it was dying.

All the bottle bombs were gone, but the team didn't need them. Not this time.

They were all thinking the same thing. The snow-plow weighed five tons—two of them courtesy of its huge V-plow. All they needed to do was hit the tank with enough force to push it into the bay and then watch it drown.

No one wanted to get out; no one wanted to miss the end of the story. Jackson revved the engine and threw the plow into gear. They started forward . . .

But then suddenly the cab was filled with the bright crimson light. It blinded them for a moment, its eerie red glow once again illuminating the Old Seabury side of the bay. Jackson hit the brakes.

The light started flashing again, but Starr didn't need to read the Morse code this time. He immediately turned on his old flip phone. Its battery icon showed empty, but it rang right away.

It was Angel, excited and once more speaking very fast.

"We're back up in the lighthouse," she reported. "And I got some more weird stuff for you. It turns out one person actually refused to be evacuated from the town. He's some kind of insurance bigwig, a top exec who has connections to the lawyer and the judge whose houses were shelled."

"No way!" Starr exclaimed.

"Way!" she exclaimed back. "Isn't that strange? This guy had to be forcibly removed from his home by the police. He's a real jerk. He didn't care what had happened to the lawyer and the judge. He's going to sue Cook and everyone else for taking him from his home—on Christmas Eve! What does that tell you?"

"That he has something hidden there that he doesn't want to leave behind," Starr said.

"Money?" she asked.

"Or drugs, or a stolen piece of artwork. Or jewelry. Or blackmail tapes and material. You know how these guys are. They're always hiding something."

"Well, he's in custody at the moment," she said. "Before coming back to the lighthouse, Cookie and I checked and re-checked the houses around this guy's place and no one is within five blocks of the area. The police force here is doing an outstanding job."

She paused a moment to catch her breath and then asked: "You're OK, right?"

"I am," Starr replied, adding: "And I hate to say this, honey, but can I call you back?"

Starr asked Jackson to put the snowplow back into neutral.

"Slight change of plans," he told the team. "But cover me, will you?"

He got out of the truck and walked down the snowy street towards the smoking tank. He had his Glock with him, but that was it.

Using the handle of the pistol, he started banging against the side of the M1. He could hear someone moving around inside. Suddenly a second hatch atop of the turret opened up.

"Come in," Starr heard a voice say.

He climbed up on the turret and peered inside—only to find another double barrel shotgun looking back at him. Its owner was deep in shadow.

"Are you the cops?" the voice asked.

"Nope—I'm with Navy," Starr replied.

He had his ID out and held it out for the man to see.

The shotgun disappeared and a hand came up out of the darkness. Elderly, smeared with grease. And some blood.

"Army," the voice said, shaking Starr's hand weakly. "Thirty-two years in armor."

"I'm not surprised to hear that," Starr told him calmly. "But we have a problem here, Army."

"I know," the voice replied. "I know I've caused a lot of trouble. But it wasn't for no reason."

"Tell me then," Starr replied.

The man cleared his raspy throat.

"You know what it's like for a career lifer like me," he said. "My wife followed me around to every god forsaken post on this planet. Every single day of those thirty-three years, she was at my side. And then she got sick. And when it came time to treat her, our insurance would not pay for what she needed. The first time they claimed the treatment was too experimental. Then because it took us so long to prove it wasn't, they claimed her condition had become too far gone to pay for something so expensive.

"Turns out, a lawyer, a judge and an insurance bigwig colluded not just on her case but on many others too, to rule in favor of the insurance company. They conspired to reject payments for patients outright and made millions in percentages from the insurance company as a reward. All of it was illegal, of course.

"They were caught and prosecuted—but they were found innocent on a technicality. So they got to go free and keep all their money, and I got to bury my lovely wife years before her time.

"When I found out they all owned houses in Old Seabury, I just couldn't let it go." The man paused for what sounded like a painful, wheezing breath.

"Have I killed any innocent people over there?" he asked Starr.

"Not yet," Starr told him. "They've evacuated the town. As for the lawyer and the judge, well . . . both are still breathing."

He heard a sigh come from below.

Starr quickly added: "But you did flatten their houses. You did a great job of that. You and your tank. Where did you get it?"

"Can you believe on eBay?" the man replied wistfully. "It's a real early model. I bought it from a war surplus dealer in Egypt, had it stripped down and the parts shipped over here, one at a time, in crates marked 'Car Parts.' I put them in a storage facility up near Weymouth, then I rented that old UFO place. I gradually brought the parts over here and put them together. I welded every piece of this baby myself. It took two years, working on it every day, with a lot of car jacks and a chain lift. It's just barely a tank now—it's more of a hobby kit. And boy did it leak gasoline. Always did. But I thought of my wife every minute of every day that I worked on it. So, it was worth it."

A flashlight came on and for the first time Starr saw the face of the man he was talking to. He was nothing like he'd imagined. He was frail, literally a bag of bones.

Starr suddenly understood. The man was dying as well.

"I'm very sorry for all the trouble I caused you," the guy went on. "I didn't want to hurt you guys or anyone really. It was just those three that needed payback. Well, at least I put the hurt on two of them. I'm hoping their insurance companies screw them—there's a good chance they will . . ."

He looked into his ammo bay. There was one round left.

"But that rat bastard insurance guy is going to get away in a breeze," the old Army vet moaned. "And he's the one that deserved it the most. And I got his house all lined up too. I should have pulled the trigger when I had a chance. Instead you guys set me on fire—and then, well, you just wouldn't leave me alone."

The sickly man looked around the interior of the tank. It was a mess of oily rags, grease, and empty Coke cans. And it did smell mightily of gasoline.

Starr finally put his gun away. He knew there'd be no need for it here.

"Well, Navy," the old guy said. "Time to surrender I guess."

He started to crawl out of the tank, then added: "Though I know I'll be lucky to make it to the hospital. I'm on my last legs. I can feel it."

That's when Starr stopped him from climbing out.

"Take your time, Army," he said. "And do what you have to do. We're not in any hurry, not anymore."

Starr saluted him. Then he closed the hatch, slowly climbed down from the tank and walked back to the others.

They were hugely curious about what was going on, but Starr just signaled that all was okay. No sooner had he done so, when the tank's turret turned and its cannon rose one last time. Then there was a tremendous roar and the ground beneath them shook wildly again. They were able to see the last shell go screaming across the bay and explode in the distance.

That was followed by the sound of a single gunshot coming from within the tank.

Then everything was quiet again.

Even the storm.

Chapter Twenty-Six

Thanks to the storm and its aftermath, the party at Angel's parents' house lasted the entire week.

Starr missed about a day and a half, but at her father's insistence, he had to make up for the lost time.

There were many occasions in those following days that Starr could have done with just a beer; he was a little off the high-priced booze after his adventure on the island.

But "Dad" was dad and so they went through three bottles of Johnnie Walker Blue in those long, foggy five days.

It was enough whisky to last Starr a lifetime.

He and Angel left New Year's Day and headed back for the Coast.

They had agreed not to discuss the details of what happened on the island while they were at her parents' house—so that's all they talked about on the ride home.

Angel knew most of the story by now. And she'd met most of the key players. She'd been there the next morning when the team returned to Old Seabury, courtesy of a Coast Guard helicopter. Jackson, Coward, Norman, the

Taylor boys and Jerry the bartender, she even met the three models.

She never laid eyes on the bar's wealthy patrons, though. Their luxury cars flattened and wanting to avoid publicity, the patrons hired their own helicopters to take them off the island.

While the townspeople flocked back to their homes in time to celebrate Christmas, the state police and the military finally arrived and closed the island to all civilians. An investigation into the affair began immediately, but any cleanup would have to wait until spring.

Starr and the team members had felt the need to see the houses the tank destroyed. Cook piled them into the town's tiny paddy wagon and drove them to the sites where he and Angel acted as their guides. The third mansion—owned by the insurance company executive—had been vaporized, just like the other targets. The exec himself was in jail, charged with assaulting one of Cookie's cops during his forced evacuation. The judge was suddenly homeless—and friendless. Word had gotten around that the guy was a moving target and no one in the town would take him in. As for the lawyer, he was still in the hospital.

When the tour was over, Angel posed for cell phone pictures with the team members and the models and they said goodbye to Chief Cook.

Then they all went their separate ways, each with a Christmas story for the ages.

"By the way, did we ever find out the tank guy's name?" Angel asked about halfway into their journey home.

"Nope," Starr replied. "He never told me, and I don't think Cookie ever knew."

"I think it's better that we don't know," she said. "That way he's an Everyman, fighting against all these dishonest institutions we have around us these days. Plus, it's more romantic that way."

"Really?" he asked.

"Of course," she told him. "It was a crazy idea, but he only did it because he loved his wife so much and she was taken from him. And he fought back. He did it all for her. That's very gallant. Women love that . . . ."

"I'll keep that in mind," Starr replied.

It took just two days to get home; average speed 90 mph. As Starr's pre-cog abilities and his NILE ID usually got him out of any tickets, he did all the driving.

By the week following their trip, things had returned to normal for Starr and Angel. Or at least normal for them.

Angel did a bunch of shoots up in LA; Starr busted a rear admiral and two of his staff for trying to sell satellite secrets to Pakistan.

One night, Angel came home after a runway show in Brentwood. Starr saw her limo arrive and slipped through the wormhole. They met in her bedroom.

She showered and put on an old ripped t-shirt. It was Starr's favorite.

"I did some intelligence gathering today," she told him, drying her hair with a towel.

He was already sprawled on the giant bed. It was a funny thing for her to say.

"How so, my flower?" he asked.

"Do you remember, Tami, Tina and Trish?"

"How could I forget? 'Three plucky models, hoping for their big break in the Big City, run into an Abrams battle tank instead.' It writes itself."

"Well, I always thought they looked a familiar. You know I can't forget a face, especially in my business. So . . . ."

She was holding two photographs fresh off a printer. The paper stock was yellow with red stripes, common for transmitting sensitive materials.

Starr's eyes narrowed to slits. "Have you been going on my secure laptop again? Angel—I've told you, that's against the law. *Federal law*. The Patriot Act. I could go to jail and . . ."

But she waved his concerns away. "You worry too much," she said sweetly. "Besides, I used my own sources to get these."

"Your own sources? Does Cosmos have its own spy network now?"

"You'd be surprised," she replied mysteriously.

She sat next to him. "Remember the picture we all took together back at Old Seabury? Well, I put that through my agency's database on Facial Recognition Search . . ."

He gently interrupted her, mildly astonished. "Your model agency has facial recognition software?"

"That's top secret," she said, again brushing away his concerns. "Just look at what popped up . . ."

She handed him the first picture.

It showed a group of female soldiers, in uniform, doing cutesy, seductive poses on a beach.

"That's from a 'Real Female Warriors' layout in Euro-Cosmo a few years ago," she said. "One of our regular photographers did the session with them. Those girls were military at one time. Take a closer look . . ."

He did and quickly realized that Tami, Tina and Trish were among the female soldiers.

"Very smart on their part, I guess," he said, never once suspecting the three girls had been military. "Get your faces out there in circulation, right?"

"In most cases, yes . . ." she replied.

Then she handed him the second photograph. "But this also popped up."

This was a news photo of a chaotic crowd scene. It showed at least a dozen people acting as bodyguards for some dignitary. Many of the faces in the photograph were blurry, but at least three were recognizable.

Tami, Tina and Trish.

"That picture was taken last year outside the U.S. Embassy in Jerusalem during a religious protest," she told him. "You should know the guy being escorted. He's the Director of Israeli Intelligence."

Starr studied the picture again and indeed recognized the man. And Tami, Tina and Trish—in plain clothes, but with guns drawn—were hustling him to his car.

"What the heck is this about?" he asked, sitting up. "They don't have just anyone protecting this guy . . ."

"Something else must have been going on out on that island," Angel told him. "Because I'm guessing your three 'models' actually work for the Mossad."

Book Three

<u>Bombardment, Inc.</u>

Chapter One

The Hoko Bokos were an army of Muslim radicals who controlled large parts of the East African country of Zuwanda.

Their name meant "holy protectors of the people," but their modus operandi was to kidnap women and girls all over the country and force the Zuwandan government to pay for their release. It was a criminal enterprise hiding under the veil of religion, and it was making the Hoko Bokos a lot of money.

At more than a thousand strong, the gang had four base camps hidden inside Zuwanda. Depending on what part of the country they planned to target next, roughly half their army would bivouac in one of these camps and use it as a launching pad for their kidnapping sprees. A few days of victimizing local villages would follow, the gang transporting their hostages to a secret location somewhere even deeper in the jungle. Then they would move on to another base and start the process all over again.

They did all this with impunity. Zuwanda was a tiny country and so poor, it couldn't afford an army, relying on its National Military Police instead. But aside from acting as go-betweens in the hostage-for-ransom

exchanges, the NMP had been wildly ineffective in trying to stop the Hoko Bokos. They showed little interest
in taking on the heavily armed, thuggish gang.

The largest Boko camp was near Tbango Falls in
northeast Zuwanda.

The country was only the size of Rhode Island, yet
some of the heaviest forests in Africa were found here.
Hidden beneath an exceptionally thick jungle canopy,
Boko Base Tbango consisted of an armory, a command
center and five temporary barracks, enough to house 500
fighters. There was also a truck park for the gang's small
fleet of technicals, Toyota pickups with heavy machine
guns installed in the back.

The Bokos reputation was one of ruthless excess, but
they were also military savvy. They would routinely es-
tablish three rings of security around whatever base they
were using, positions manned with even more heavy machine guns. The Bokos also had two Buk-M2 SAM missile launchers and a state of the art 1L-122 anti-aircraft
radar dish. Anything from jet fighters to helicopters to
cruise missiles and even drones could be shot down by
these missiles.

Bum Hokumi was the leader of the Bokos gang. Late
40s, big and bald, he'd become very wealthy lately. He'd
made more than $12 million in ransoms in just the past

year, virtually bleeding the anemic Zuwandan government dry. And as he never faced any opposition, there was no reason to doubt his scam could go on for years.

He and his men had been encamped at Tbango Falls for two days now, raiding villages nearby. Sunset brought an end to this day's operations and those fighters with night duty reported to their stations. All unnecessary fires were doused; blackout rules went into effect. Any off duty soldiers were told to get a good night's sleep. It would all begin again at dawn.

Once their evening prayers were finished, Bum and his officers gathered inside his portable command center for their evening meal. Roasted red colobus, dried boli and pepper soup were delicacies in this part of the world, but this was a celebration. In just the past 48 hours, the gang had snatched ninety-seven women and girls from the local villages, immediately sending them back to the gang's secret stash house. As Bum's ransom demands were usually $2500 per hostage, he could expect to get nearly a quarter million dollars just for these victims alone.

To further mark the occasion, he opened a bottle of cognac, a forbidden pleasure among the jihadists. But just as he was pouring, he suddenly held up his hand, signaling for quiet.

He cocked his ear skyward.

"Do you hear something?" he asked.

Chapter Two

Chris Starr awoke with a start.

Angel was sitting next to him, reading a Vogue.

"Did you hear that?" he asked her.

"Not unless I was in your dream," she said, turning the page.

Starr scanned his surroundings. They were on an airplane. Private cabin. British Airways. Flying to . . . the UAE. Angel was doing a show there.

"When did I go to sleep?"

She continued flipping through the magazine. "Thirty seconds after we left."

He barely remembered taking off. It had been a whirlwind week. Angel had done the Met Gala in New York City three nights before. Then there was a shoot in London yesterday. Next stop: Dubai.

She closed the magazine and gently stroked his brow.

"Bad dream, my prince?" she asked sweetly.

"I'm not sure," he replied.

He could still hear the strange sound that knocked him awake. Like a million firecrackers going off at once.

A flight attendant appeared at their door. "About twenty minutes to landing," she told them. Then she handed Starr a portable radio phone, taking the time to pull out its telescoping antenna first.

"And Lieutenant Starr? You have an inflight call from Mister Hooper . . ."

Angel's heart sank. "Oh no. Not him again?"

Their plane arrived at Dubai International twenty-one minutes later.

The flight crew escorted the other passengers out of ultra-class before coming for Angel and Starr. She signed a few copies of Elle for the attendants and then they were led out to the tarmac through the plane's rear door.

Starr's conversation with "Mister Hooper" had been brief. Naval Intelligence Operations in DC had tracked him down. He was needed elsewhere.

He kissed Angel for a long time, a fog blowing off the Persian Gulf enveloping them in gloom.

"I'm so sorry about this," he told her.

"You know I usually don't mind," she said, her eyes starting to water. "But I've been looking forward to this for so long. The Garavani collection is the biggest show I've ever done. Plus it's our seven-month anniversary. I packed the superheroes costumes and everything."

"I will be there," Starr told her without hesitation.

He sounded so certain, she was a little shocked. "Are you sure?"

"When is your Garavani spot?"

"Sunday afternoon, one o'clock, their time . . ."

Starr punched the buttons on his Smart Watch and got the display counting backwards to Sunday 1:00 p.m. local time, 40 hours away.

He showed her the digits running in reverse. "I promise I'll be back in time to see your Garavani spot."

She hugged him tightly. "Please be careful . . ."

"You too," he told her, but his words were drowned out by the roar of a jet airplane taxing over to them. It was a U.S. Marine Corps F-18F Super Hornet. The all-black two-seat fighter appeared out of the mist, approaching from a military runway close by.

The jet stopped in front of them, its canopy went up and the pilot gave Starr a quick salute.

One more kiss—then Starr climbed the retractable ladder and squeezed himself into the fighter's rear seat. He waved to Angel just as a limo arrived to pick her up. She blew him a kiss, but it was lost in the fog.

The Hornet pilot closed the canopy and made a right turn back onto the military runway. Then he went to full power and lifted them off into the night.

Chapter Three

About three quarters of Zuwanda was jungle, a small but hellish desert took up the rest.

There was only one oasis in its three hundred square miles of sand and desolation, a mudhole called Mubago Drift. But it was in this unlikely spot that the U.S. Navy SEALs had built a small forward operating base called OB16—Oasis Base, SEAL Team 16.

The base was a classic example of hiding in plain sight. A marvel in camouflage, from the air it looked like an abandoned village sitting next to a puddle and a few palm trees. Dug out below it, though, was a subterranean facility that could accommodate a thirty-man SEAL detachment team and all their gear. Numerous top-secret missions in East Africa had been launched from OB16, a place that only a handful of people in the Pentagon even knew existed.

The hidden base contained an operations center, a barracks, a communications room and a mess. Part of the ops center was devoted to air traffic control, for next to the ersatz village was a dry lakebed runway that could handle anything up to a C-130 cargo plane. Supply flights came in twice a month, always in the dead of night.

The equipment needed to tend visiting aircraft was hidden underground as well. Not that it mattered. Located twenty miles from the edge of Zuwanda's jungle, OB16 had been here for six years and no human had ever tripped its security system.

The lakebed runway was equipped with infrared lighting and an arrestor hook; that's how Starr's F-18F taxi was able to land.

The pilot stopped long enough for him to climb out, then he turned the fighter jet around and cranked its engines back to high. He gave Starr a wave and hit the afterburner. The F-18F did a quick takeoff roll and then ascended straight up until it disappeared into the stars.

Starr was met by two SEALs who escorted him over to the fake village. It was almost 2000 hours—8 p.m. local time—but still very hot. However, by the time Starr got in the facility's tiny, hand-operated elevator and went down to the underground operations room, the temperature had dropped by 40 degrees. The SEALs had some kick-ass air conditioning in their desert hutch.

The team's detachment commander met him at the elevator door. He was Captain Mike Fong, a rugged, tatted Asian-American right out of central casting. They walked the short distance to the ops room where Fong's four-person staff was waiting. But as soon as Starr was introduced around, these people excused themselves and left.

"This is an extremely sensitive matter, lieutenant," Fong told him. "The fewer involved, the better."

A 55-inch TV was suspended above the room's planning table. Fong clicked a remote and its screen came to life.

"I assume you're familiar with the NRO's Topaz-8 Program?" he asked Starr.

Starr nodded. The NRO was the National Reconnaissance Office; it operated all of America's spy satellites. Many of its space-based peeping toms took pictures or shot video. Topaz-8 was different. Its eight satellites used radar imaging to detect objects on the Earth's surface and present them in incredibly precise detail. And unlike other types of spy satellites, Topaz-8 could do this through cloud cover or darkness—or, as it turned out, the thick jungle canopy that covered so much of Zuwanda.

"A Topaz-8 being recalibrated in low orbit caught this about a day ago," Fong told him, once again clicking the remote.

At first, the footage showed only a thick patch of jungle. But as the camera zoomed in, it switched on its radar imaging function and suddenly Starr could see a very large military camp hidden beneath the forest overhang. Lots of weapons, lots of armed vehicles, lots of armed men. The base wasn't invisible like OB16, but as camouflage went, it was a pretty good job.

"Ever hear of the Hoko Boko?" Fong now asked him.

Starr nodded again. "Religious-extremist terrorist organization?" he said. "Hybrid of Nigeria's Boko Haram and Somalia's Hoko Mijam. Upstarts, but with above-average weaponry."

"That's them," Fong said. "They've been active inside Zuwanda for about a year. And, officially at least, this is the first time one of their bases has been picked up by our secret squirrels. The jungle is very heavy in this part of Africa and, like us, the 'Hobos' know how to hide themselves."

He froze the image on the screen for a moment.

"They make their money through kidnappings," he explained. "But they've also got the Zuwandan government by the balls. They wanted to operate freely inside the country without interference from anyone, including the United States. And in exchange for releasing a hundred hostages a few months ago, that's exactly what they got—a full hall pass, even though they're still holding about five hundred hostages somewhere.

"Now, the Zuwandan president lets us have our clubhouse out here in return for a secret payment from the CIA every year. But we also had to agree not to operate inside his country, as he thinks that would be the quickest way for him to get caught with his hand in Uncle Sam's pants. So, our little place here is simply a subway stop. We can do no military ops, no intelligence gathering, nothing within the borders of Zuwanda, and technically, nothing above it either. If the U.S. gets caught violating this secret agreement, they can kick us out."

He started the image moving again.

"That said, you are looking at a place called Tbango Falls. It's one of four camps the Hobos are believed to have inside the country."

Fong pointed to a highlighted section of the base.

"Thanks to Mother Russia, they've got SAM launchers and an above-average anti-aircraft warning system," he went on. "Any kind of air strike on this place would be risky. And as you can see, they've got enough firepower to fight off a sizable ground attack too. Between all this, and the money they've already squeezed out of the Zuwandan government, these guys were sitting pretty."

"'Were?'" Starr asked.

Fong ended the first imaging loop and started a second one. "This was taken very early this morning. You'll see why the NRO went back to take a quick peek."

It showed the same satellite image, from the same angle, looking down at the same piece of Zuwandan forest. But the jungle canopy was gone—and so was the

Hoko Boko camp. It had been obliterated. There was nothing left but scorched earth.

Starr whistled softly. "What the hell did that?"

"I'd love to say a low yield tactical nuke," Fong confessed. "Only because it would be a lot easier to figure out."

The level of destruction *was* astonishing. But there was another odd thing: The resulting scar on the ground had a very unusual shape.

"Not only was this place wiped out," Fong told him, "but the footprint of the destruction is, let's call it, unconventional."

It was true. That footprint—more than three football fields long and half that wide—was in the shape of a near-perfect rectangle. Its corners seemed to be impeccably squared off.

"I've never seen anything like that," Starr said.

"No one has," Fong replied. "And I'm guessing that's why they instructed the Topaz-8 to take another look at it, on the QT."

The SEAL commander shut off the TV and poured two cups of coffee. He gave one to Starr.

"So, any idea who gave those guys their haircut?" he asked the SEAL CO, adding six artificial creamers and lots of sugar to his cup.

Fong shook his head. "All we know right now is who *didn't* do it. First of all—it wasn't us. Believe me, we never raise our heads out here, plus we could never be that tidy. And because the Hobos had that air-warning system, it wasn't an air raid or anybody's cruise missiles. That would have been a battle and we would have heard the racket up here, fifty miles away."

"How about the Zuwandan Army?"

Fong laughed darkly. "It doesn't exist," he said. "The closest thing the Zuwandans have is the NMP—the National Military Police. But they're bunch of losers."

"How so?"

Fong lowered his voice. "We don't gather intel inside Zuwanda, but that doesn't mean things don't come our way. About nine months ago, the NMP made a big splash about ambushing some Hobos and rescuing a bunch of hostages. Only problem was, someone sent Langley photos of the NMP soldiers coming back from this operation and their uniforms aren't even wrinkled. Their pants were still creased, their hands were still clean and none of them had even broken a sweat. Make no mistake, the kidnap victims looked severely traumatized—and, the photo shrinks say—sexually abused. The NMP guys looked like they were just coming back from lunch.

"And since then, the NMP has done little more than act as go betweens in these hostage-for-ransom releases that happen every once in a while. The cops hand over the money, the Hobos hand over the victims and that's it. The idea that they'd actually take them on in a gunfight is ludicrous. Bottom line: they're not the ones who put the hurt on the Hobos."

Starr added more sugar to his coffee. "Okay—how about a rival gang with a lot of weaponry? Eliminate the competition, move in and take over the kidnapping scam. Could it be as simple as that?"

Fong shrugged. "Anything is possible in this fucked up little country. But when you look at the extent of the destruction, it seems unlikely another gang would have that much firepower and especially the ability to use it so exactly."

He refilled their cups, and then lowered his voice even further.

"But whatever happened, a lot of political bullshit has come down as a result," he said. "Some people close to the Zuwandan president are telling him that *we* hit the Hobos without consulting them. Now if he really comes to believe that, then he can tear up the secret agreement about having us in his country. We've been informed through channels that unless we can tell him definitively within the next forty-eight hours who hit the Hobos, he's going to assume it was us and we'll have to pack our bags and go."

He took a breath and then said: "That's why you're here, lieutenant. You have to find out what happened before the Zuwandans pull the plug. Your friends at Naval Intelligence tell us that figuring out the impossible is what you do. I really hope that's the case because we're sitting on a box of hand grenades here and all the pins are about to fall out. If we have to go somewhere else, everything from Africa Command to Gulf Command will feel the pain.

"So, please do what you do and solve this as quickly—and as quietly—as possible."

Chapter Four

One hour later

Starr stole out of the SEALs base and trudged over to the salt flats runway.

It was now 2100, 9:00 p.m. local time. His Smart Watch seemed to be counting down at an impossibly fast rate. Now he faced *two* deadlines: one to solve the Hobo mystery and one to get back in time for Angel's show.

He was wearing a SEAL combat suit, courtesy of Commander Fong. It included a vest with armor body plates, an oversized helmet equipped with interactive night vision goggles and a "super-ear" app, which allowed him to hear any sounds below him, including voices. He also had a pair of bolt cutters, a package of chem-lights and five Snickers bars.

For protection, Fong issued him an M4 HK rifle with bayonet—standard cutlery for the SEALs—a .45 automatic pistol and a shot suppressor that could be used on both.

It sounded like a lot to carry, but this was the SEALs latest kit; it weighed less than twenty pounds, including the weaponry. That would be a plus.

He put his ear to the wind and heard the dull rumble of an airplane approaching.

"Right on time," he thought.

It was an old C-47, one of a bunch still flying. Coming at him full throttle, just 200 feet off the deck, he saw a side door open and a box tumble out. The plane roared overhead and was out of sight almost before the package hit the ground.

Starr retrieved the bundle; a shipping label was attached: "One PAV-478 vehicle. Requisitioned NILE station/Ethiopia. Lieutenant C. Starr. You are responsible for the contents of this package." It was stamped: "East Ghana Air Delivery Service"

He ripped open the bundle to find a large duffle bag. Inside *that* was the PAV-478.

It was an airplane. A very small, *inflatable* airplane. The wings, the fuselage and the tail section were all separate units. Fill them with air from the accompanying pump, brace them with guy wires, attach the small electric propeller and you were off. It couldn't fly faster than 70 mph and no higher than 250 feet. But it was near silent, and because of its dull, light-dispersing material, it was almost invisible day or night.

Basically it was a human stealth drone.

Perfect for what Starr had to do.

He was airborne twenty minutes later.

In flight, the PAV was more blimp than airplane. It rarely flew in a straight line, riding the winds like a motorboat rides the waves. But it was stable enough, and astonishingly quiet.

Fong had given him a thumb drive that contained a collage of old satellite photos, among other things. Plugging the drive into his interactive night vision goggles, Starr was able to follow this collage as a moving map, complete with updated coordinates. Using it as a guide, he turned southwest from OB16, and headed for Tbango Falls, fifty miles away.

Flying over Africa at night was a first for him. Aided by the NVGs he could see dots of light—from fires, from houses and villages—scattered across the landscape below him. There was a certain beauty to this place, haunting and, through his NVGs, electronically emerald.

He spotted the remains of the Hobo camp about forty minutes later.

The image collage led him right to the enormous rectangle carved into the deep jungle. He went down to 100 feet, did one wide circle, reconning the place via night vision. Once certain that no one else was in the area, he set down the PAV for a typically bumpy landing.

He walked the entire perimeter of the devastated area, raising clouds of white ash with every step. Even up close, the rectangular hole in the jungle looked almost exact, with nearly all straight lines and sharp corners.

The SEALs were right. This was no cruise missile strike. Tomahawks left big, deep craters; there were no such depressions here. But it hadn't been a gunship or helicopter attack either. They left a moonscape of thousands of little craters, and again, this did not fit the bill.

Artillery? Not of any caliber Starr could think of.

Rail gun? Kinetic weapons? Lasers? Something else even more exotic, shot from space? Considering who the target was, Starr doubted anyone would risk revealing such an ultra top secret weapon on a bunch of thugs like the Hobos. And, as Fong said, if this was the doing of a rival jihadist gang, where in the world would they get firepower like this?

Starr tried to stoke the recesses of his pre-cog, begging the Cosmos to give him something—anything—to point him in the right direction. But nothing came, as if the part of his brain that gave him his ESP abilities was as stumped as the rest of him.

Finally, he stepped over the boundary of the huge scar and took a few steps into the jungle beyond. That's when he noticed something else: the trees along the edge of the devastated area were virtually unchanged; many were still standing tall and were unsinged.

He looked up at the stars. Whatever happened here, he thought, whatever destroyed this place, came straight down.

He reached for his phone two seconds before it began buzzing.

It was Fong.

"Some new real estate has just opened up south of you," the SEAL commander told him. "See my text."

Fong hung up and his text arrived an instant later. It was a set of coordinates for a place called Wandinga Ridge. It said something unusual had been spotted there not by an NRO satellite but, at least as told to Fong, by one belonging to the National Weather Service.

Starr was back in the air two minutes later, the flattened if dusty earth providing a bouncy but workable runway for the PAV.

Climbing back to 250 feet, he found the wind was with him. He called up Fong's coordinates on his interactive NVGs and then did a long slow turn due south. Twenty minutes later, he was more than 30 miles away from Tbango Falls and approaching the Wandinga River.

Turning his NVGs up to full power, he detected a massive heat source rising just ahead of him. A minute later he was over a bluff sitting next to a bend in the river itself. According to a map contained on the thumb drive, a long-abandoned cattle ranch was located under the jungle cover here—but no more. There was some smoke and some flames and the skeletal remains of some Toyota trucks could be seen. But few other things remained on the bluff now, including what he had to assume were at least a hundred Hobo fighters.

Judging by the smoldering fires, Starr guessed the place had been hit no more than an hour ago.

And just like before, there was an enormous scar on the ground in the shape of a near-perfect rectangle.

"How the hell do they do that?" he wondered out loud.

Chapter Five

Starr flew for the rest of the night and into the next day.

North to south, east and west, back and forth. He traced and retraced a grid pattern all over tiny Zuwanda, suddenly desperate to find any sign of the two remaining Hobo camps.

Because of the no-interference agreement with the Zuwandan president, U.S. intelligence didn't know where the other bases were, or if they did, they sure weren't telling anyone. So Starr was searching for something that America's best spy satellites weren't allowed to look for. Such was his life.

But it got even more complicated, another life trait of his. Not only did he need to locate at least one of the camps, he had to be there *while* it was being attacked. At this point, that was the only way to find out who was decimating the Hobos and doing so at a rapid pace.

But . . . if he was able to do that, if he was able to solve this mystery, his job would be done. Whoever the culprit was, he would get an ID on them, then kick it all upstairs before the Zuwandan president went nuts, and *still* get back in time to see Angel's show.

Or at least that was the plan. But so far, he was batting zero.

This was where his precognitive gifts were supposed to come into play. This was why he was in NILE in the first place. Yet after hours of nonstop flying, he'd accomplished nothing more than giving himself a sore butt. It was a brutally hot day and the constant thermal updrafts made for an endlessly jarring flight. His eyes were peeled to see anything—a recently used path, a puff of smoke, lots of tire tracks—*anything* that would indicate a base was close by. He'd also used the super-ear app in his NVG set extensively, hoping to hear a large group of people on the move, or a random bit of military chatter.

But as the hours dragged on, his Snickers supply dwindled and his smart watch continued to tick down and he kept coming up empty.

When he wasn't flying over the thick forest, he was traversing the Kikiwalla Highway, which Starr was sure in Zuwandan meant "dangerous winding road that sometimes straightens out into a mad speedway for large trucks." The serpentine highway was the country's aortic artery. Everything moving north and south used this road and he'd seen multiple traffic accidents involving trucks either misjudging the dangerous curves or going way too fast on its handful of straightaways.

But he felt no buzz from any of it.

Shortly after 3:00 p.m., he'd flown over the field headquarters of Zuwanda's National Military Police.

It was located at the dead center of the country, in the middle of nowhere. At first Starr thought he was looking at a five-star hotel right out of Boca Raton. There were a handful of white and bleached buildings, two swimming pools, several bowling greens, a golf course, a tennis court, an enormous horse barn and a series of corrals that looked elaborate enough to train thoroughbred horses. There was also a sizable airport nearby that the NMP bigwigs used to come and go.

Starr could see a few dozen people about the place. Many were lounging by the pools. Others were catching a snooze in a colorful array of beach chairs. Still others were seated under large umbrellas, playing cards.

Most all he could hear via the super-ear app was loud music from a radio, the sounds of a game of Sink-Sink being played, some horses' baying and snoring.

He was sure if he drew closer he would see that none of the NMP cops had lost the crease in their pants today.

Night fell.

His last Snickers was gone, his Smart watch kept ticking down, and his butt was numb. But he kept on flying because he couldn't think of anything else to do.

Discouragement was the number one enemy for any investigator, and Starr could feel it creeping up on him. He looked up at the sky full of stars. More stars than not. And only the thinnest wisp of the crescent moon. And a thought suddenly popped into his head . . . he wondered if Angel was looking up at the moon at that very moment and wouldn't it be cool if he could bounce his thoughts off the lunar surface and have them come back down to her.

It was an odd, almost childish notion.

But a moment later, his pre-cog finally kicked in.

It started only as a brief flash, but that was all he needed at the moment.

He turned south, the wind in his favor again. He was swept along 250 feet above the jungle, everything moving in slightly fast motion, always a good sign. From below he could hear hundreds of bird calls and animal sounds blending with the wind, whizzing by his ears. It sounded almost symphonic.

He flew like this for thirty miles, trying to keep his nose pointed dead south. Once he passed the outskirts of the Zuwandan capital of Kahpala, he pulled back on his speed, and went down to 100 feet. Then he put the night vision goggles on high, engaged the enhanced infrared record function—and found a Hobo base right below him.

He recognized it by the three rings of heavy machine guns, the row of technicals and the crude wooden barracks. His talent for using the powers of the Great Beyond had paid off again.

But then he felt a shiver go through him, a bolt of electricity shaking him from helmet to boots. A second later, he saw a single flash of light, rising into the sky right in front of him.

Then came another flash, same location, climbing quickly from the jungle.

Then another.

And another.

Suddenly there was an explosion of light. It flooded his night vision goggles to the point he could feel it burning his retinas.

Just like that, the sky around him became lit up like daytime. *Hundreds* of streaks of blazing light were now shooting up from the deep jungle.

And they looked like fireworks.

Again? he thought.

Then came another message from beyond.

Hold on . . .

The shock wave hit him a second later. It knocked the PAV out of its flight envelope, putting it into a stall.

Suddenly Starr was upside down and heading towards the ground. He kept his cool though. One goose of the power switch stopped the engine burping, resuming its familiar buzz. He slammed the controls to the left and then jerked them back into his lap.

A second later he was upright and level again.

But in the next moment, he looked up to see the first waves of light had reached their apogees. And just that quickly, they began falling back to Earth—and coming right at him.

He jammed the controls to the right, almost stalling again. This was getting serious now—whatever *this* was. He went down to treetop level, trying to stay ahead of the descending barrage. That's when he glanced down at the jungle . . .

And this was when it really got weird because at that instant, his video-graphic memory suddenly kicked in. He instantly went to pause. One moment he was in fast motion, the next, everything came to a screeching halt.

In this freeze frame he saw the streaks of light were being launched from a platform right below him—a very unusual one. It was a double tractor trailer truck parked in a section of jungle that had been hacked down to accommodate its size. Nearby was a towed water tank.

On the back of the extended tractor trailer was an array of six gigantic . . . mortars. Starr immediately recognized them as Russian made 240mm M20 *Tyulpans*.

A breath caught in his throat. These were truly terrifying weapons. They fired a shell that contained a hundred pounds of cluster munitions. Just one of these shells could saturate an area the size of an American football field. With dozens timed to hit the target in continuous waves, the combined detonation would result in a massive explosion.

He started the mental image rolling again. The strange gun platform was crowded with men wearing face masks and camo uniforms. But they were moving like a pit crew at a Formula-1 car race, their well-drilled choreography enabling one shell per mortar be launched every three seconds. At that rate, times six, more than a hundred of the gigantic shells could be fired in less than a minute.

This was definitely not some rival gang of thugs eliminating the Hobos as their competition. These guys were highly trained, had sophisticated weaponry and knew how to handle vast amounts of firepower.

So who were they?

Starr slipped back to reality. He'd flown only a couple hundred feet while under the VGM spell, but his mind was still racing.

Back in 2014, Luhansk Airport in the Ukraine. The Russian Army bombarded the place with just two *Tyulpans,* causing such widespread destruction, the CIA and others thought at first that a tactical nuke had been dropped.

Even more chilling, the Russians used *Tyulpans* to level entire neighborhoods in the Syrian Civil War, killing thousands.

So, were the Russians now in Zuwanda?

It was at that moment that the whole bombastic volley finally came down atop the Hobo camp.

When it all hit the ground, the combined detonation looked like a tidal wave of fire symmetrically carving its way across the terrorists' base—in the shape of a near-perfect rectangle.

With his super-ear app turned all the way up, to Starr, it sounded like a million firecrackers going off at once.

Chapter Six

By the time Starr completed a wide turn above the devastated base, the double tractor trailer truck, the mortars and the mortar men had disappeared . . . at least on night vision.

But he knew they were down there, because he'd detected a faint cloud of steam rising up from the truck's former location.

These guys were smart. That's why they'd brought the towed water tank with them. Immediately after firing their final volley at the Hobo base, they'd turned water hoses on the hot mortar tubes, cooling them off and making them less conspicuous on any infrared device peeping in at them.

But they couldn't hide the wisps of mist that remained.

Starr reset his super-ear app, turned it back to full power and did a complete sweep of the area. Just west of him came the sound of big wheels crushing vegetation in the dark jungle. Then on his NVGs, a glint of orange light. It was from the mortar truck—not it's cooled off weapons, but its heating-up engine.

He flew over it seconds later. The truck was moving slowly down a hacked-out path, towing the water tank.

The crew had reattached the sides to the double trailers, making it look more like an ordinary double truck.

He watched as it snaked its way through the jungle until reaching a gravel road. With a roar from its engine, it made it up onto the rough pavement and began moving faster. After driving for a quarter mile, the truck turned left and was suddenly on the Kikiwalla Highway, Zuwanda's crazy main artery.

It steered south and began traveling at high speed. Starr tightened his seat belt and pushed his tiny electric propeller to its limit in order to keep pace with the mystery truck, certain this was the beginning of a long escape.

Suddenly the tomato can rang.

His eyes glued to the strange vehicle, Starr disconnected from the super-ear, pulled out the tiny sat dish antenna and took the call.

It was Angel.

Her voice sounded far away and, for some reason, high above him, like it was coming from heaven. But he was so glad it was her.

"Please tell me you're being careful!" she said right away.

"I am," he replied. "What about you? No incidents on the catwalk, I hope."

"Thank God, no. We're in a final run-through for the Garavani show. How's it going, whatever you're doing?"

"Up to my eyeballs in it," Starr told her.

She had a minute between outfit changes, so, as he frequently did, he gave her the basics: Someone was leveling camps belonging to the Hobos. It wasn't the U.S. military and it certainly wasn't the country's military police. Up until now, the Hobos had been the dominant armed force in Zuwanda and they were still holding about 500 hostages at a secret location somewhere in the country. But it was unlikely that some kind of rival upstart gang could just come out of nowhere and inflict so much pain on them in such a bizarre way.

"I'm tracking a very unusual weapon that just flattened another Hobo camp," he told her. "I saw the attack myself and it was crazy. Now I've got to find out who did it—and why."

"Maybe it's a love story," Angel said suddenly.

"Excuse me?"

"Maybe whoever's doing all this bombing has a loved one being held by these Hobo people. They don't know where the kidnap victims are, so they're doing the next best thing. They're attacking the Hobos themselves. It might be about someone who loves someone and is trying to get them back."

Starr almost laughed. "I guess anything's possible . . ."

He checked his Smart Watch. He had less than 20 hours to solve this monkey and get back for Angel's big show. He was about to reassure her that he'd be on time when the tomato can started beeping—and suddenly she was gone.

He tried a dozen times to get her back, but nothing worked.

Their connection was broken.

He almost threw the sat phone away, he was so angry. That's when he glanced down and saw the bombardment vehicle had pulled off the road.

He put the PAV into a screaming tight turn. When he spotted the truck again, he found himself looking down at something more at home in the American Midwest than in darkest Africa.

Chapter Seven

It was a truck stop.

Large roadhouse, gas pumps, repair shop, a small mountain of old tires. Dozens of rigs were parked in a huge lot out back.

The roadhouse was decked out in year-round Christmas lights; kitchen smoke was pouring from a half dozen stacks. And Starr didn't need the super-ear to hear the bass from the skillions music; it was shaking the PAV even up at 250 feet.

This was definitely not foreseen. He was sure he was going to follow the mystery truck for miles until it eventually reached its hiding place.

But this place was not ten miles from where the truck had just destroyed the Hobo camp.

Why stop here?

Starr landed in a field just south of the crowded parking lot. Deflating and securing the PAV took a few minutes. He tried Angel twice more in that time, but with no luck.

The racket from the roadhouse was so loud at ground level, he was sure no one here heard the Hobo base hidden nearby get wiped out. It was also getting hard to ignore the smells coming from the roadhouse's kitchen. Except for the five Snickers bars, he hadn't eaten since London.

He left the tomato can and the H&K rifle with the PAV, but took the .45 automatic with him. Slipping into the parking lot, he felt a buzzing just above his right eyebrow. He'd come to recognize this as meaning something unexpected was going to happen. It made him double check that the .45 had a full clip.

He crept along the rows of parked trucks, staying in the shadows, the hot night air now heavy with diesel fumes. It took about a minute, but he finally spotted the double trailer truck parked in a cluster of rigs at the far edge of the lot. It looked no different than the super sized lorries found all over the continent. Its purposely beat up modular sidings and dirty gray paint job only added to its masquerade.

But two things gave it away. Parts of the truck were still wet from its post action wash down. Plus, he could smell the stink of cordite leftover from launching the dozens of huge mortar shells.

He stole up to the rear bumper of the truck when the buzzing in his head went from bee to chainsaw.

Get ready to be surprised . . .

He clicked the safety off the .45.

Behind you . . .

He turned, barrel first, to find himself staring at the business end of another .45 automatic. It was being held by a large black man wearing unmarked jungle camos, a wide brim boonie hat and smoking a cigarette.

Starr's first thought: Not your typical Russian.

But then came the surprise.

"Chris?" he heard the man gasp. "Chris *Starr*?"

"Fitzy?"

They both took a step to the right and into the multi-colored light coming from the roadhouse.

Starr couldn't believe it—he knew this guy.

It was Kubwa—"Great Sailor" in ancient Swahili. Or at least that was his cryptonym. His real name was Patrick Fitzpatrick—and he was from Dublin. Fitzy to his friends, he called himself "the original Black Irishman."

Starr had first met him a couple years before during an anti-pirating operation in the Malacca Straits off Indonesia. At the time Fitzy was captain of a freighter named the *Lola Marie,* a ship that had a reputation for weapons-smuggling. In reality, he and his crew were modern day privateers. Their employer: the CIA. Langley paid them to hunt down and dispose of ocean going vessels belonging to enemies of the United States. Terrorist shipping, Iran's shadowy navy, pirates on all seven seas. Many met their end after a visit from the *Lola*

Marie. Because of Fitzy's help, the Indonesia operation ended successfully. They'd been friends ever since.

They both lowered their weapons and did a quick bro-hug. Fitzy nearly squeezed the breath out of him. Then they stepped back into the shadows.

"What the hell are you doing here, Chris?"

Starr had to laugh. "You know what I do for a living, Fitzy," he said. "So you know who has to go first."

Fitzpatrick took a deep breath; he was obviously in some distress.

"I got married since the last time we saw each other," he said. "Wife number four, but I'll tell you, she was the one."

"Was?"

Fitzy's face fell. "You know who the Hoko Bokos are?" he asked.

Starr nodded.

"They took her, Chris," Fitzy told him. "She was a nurse at a UN aid station in Samarra and those animals came into the village, shot all the men and took all the females, including my wife. I'm here trying to get her back."

The news hit Starr like a cannon shot. For his friend, this was a nightmare come true.

But . . . Angel had been right.

It *was* a love story . . .

Fitzy took out his smart phone, called up a photograph and showed it to Starr. It was of a gorgeous African woman.

"Wow," Starr murmured.

"She was taken five months ago tomorrow," Fitzy told him, running his finger along the photo. "I've been going out of my mind ever since."

"But the Hobos release people on a regular basis; that's how they make their money . . ."

Fitzy bit his lip hard. "I know—and I keep waiting. But she's never been in a group they've freed. And no one knows where they keep their hostages. I'm afraid to wonder why they're holding her so long."

Starr couldn't help but lower his voice. "What about our pals at Langley. They owe you a favor I'm sure."

Fitzy threw away his cigarette in disgust.

"I went to the U.S. consulate," he said, "hoping to get a message to them. But they wouldn't let me in the door. Then I went to the Zuwandans and tried to get a bribe to someone up in the presidential palace—but they were worse than the consulate. Once they found out why I was there, no one gave me the time of day."

"So what are you doing out here—with this?" Starr asked him, pointing to the gun truck.

"I didn't know what else to do," Fitzy said. "So I got this simple idea: If I could somehow eliminate the

Hobos, then all the hostages would be freed by default. I knew it would be a long shot, but I had nothing else to go on . . ."

"*So?*"

"So—I hired these guys."

He pulled out a small card and handed it to Starr.

It read: "Bombardment, Inc. Specializing in Heavy Mortars."

Starr couldn't believe it. "*This* is a business?"

Fitzy nodded. "And I have a contract with them."

Chapter Eight

Fitzpatrick led him through a side door and into the roadhouse.

The American vibe continued inside. The place looked like a saloon from the Old West. Long wooden bar, lots of wooden chairs and tables. Lots of guns.

Sarkodie was blasting from the DJ's speakers—until the moment Starr walked in. That's when everyone, including the DJ, stopped what they were doing and stared at him, the only white guy in the place.

Fitzy hustled him out of the doorway and into a room off the bar. Out of sight, out of mind, the place began bouncing again a second later.

About thirty men were gathered in this side room, also in unmarked combat uniforms. They were having a quick meal, while standing and no one was drinking alcohol. They were all heavily armed, but Starr could see just as many laptops as weapons.

"Ready to get your mind blown?" Fitzy half-whispered to him.

"Ready," Starr said with a nod.

Fitzy began: "During the Sixties, some of the American brothers leaving Vietnam wound up around here. Because of what was happening in your country back then, they were in no hurry to get home. A bunch of them married locals and decided to stay."

Starr was surprised. He'd heard of other post-war enclaves in Thailand and the Philippines. Vietnam vets who never went home. But Africa?

"They were good soldiers," Fitzy went on. "A lot of them became mercs and a lot of them passed down what they knew to their kids."

"Sounds like a movie," Starr said. "Two generations, soldiers of fortune."

Fitzpatrick elbowed him in the ribs. "These are their *grandkids,* Chris," he said. "When I came upon their site on the Dark Web, I cashed in everything I owned, including the *Lola Marie*, and was ready to give it all to them, if they could help me. They took the minimum. They're not in it for the money."

Now *that* was mind blowing. Mercenaries not in it for the money?

Fitzy caught the attention of one of the men and asked him to come over. He was in his early thirties, boonie hat hiding an old-style afro. Fitzgerald introduced him as Jack Nephew, commander of the bombardment truck.

"My American friend here is curious about your business," Fitzy said to Nephew with a wink. "I've told him what we've been doing, and he'd like to ask you a few questions."

They walked outside and back to the bombardment truck.

Starr began right away: "Question number one: why mortars?"

Nephew looked at Fitzy who nodded. "It's OK—he's one of us."

"They're the perfect jungle weapon," Nephew said in perfect English. "You get close to your target, you let a bunch go, they never hear them coming. Same effect as an airstrike or artillery. But with mortars, you always control the point of fire. And with multiple mortars, firing in rapid order, you can get a lot of firepower into a concentrated area."

"Question two: where did you get those Russian Tyulpans?"

Again, Nephew looked to Fitzgerald for guidance.

"Let me plead the fifth for him on that," the bearish Irishman said. "Let's just say I have friends who deal in these things."

"Okay," Starr said with a knowing glance at Fitzy. "Then how about the perfect rectangle carved into the ground?"

"Our aiming systems are keyed to GPS," Nephew replied. "Select what you want your saturation spread to be, punch it in and fire away. Our laptops do the rest."

"But it's so freaking precise," Starr said. "How is that possible?"

Fitzy explained: "Think of a building demolition. They put the explosives here and the building will fall this way. Put them over there, the building will fall the other way. Everything is coordinated, like the fireworks at Cannes, or New York Harbor on the Fourth of July."

It was all finally sinking in for Starr.

"Last question," he said. "How did you guys know where those three Hobo bases were?"

Nephew shrugged. "We have the best intel resource in the country: the people. We talk to them and they trust us. We asked them to tell us about any large or unusual fuel thefts in any area we thought the Bokos might be operating. No matter what those animals did, they always needed gas for all those technicals and it wasn't like they were going to drive into a city and just fill up. So when a lot of fuel was suddenly gone out in the countryside somewhere, we knew it was probably them and that they were on the move and we had our friends follow them. That's how we found the first three camps."

Starr allowed himself a small moment of triumph. This was all excellent to hear. With four questions, he'd solved the mystery. He now knew who'd been liquidating the Hobos, how they were doing it and why. More important, he could prove it wasn't the SEALS or anyone else connected with the U.S. military.

All he had to do now was report the info to Fong at OB-16, at which point it would become someone else's problem—and he'd make Angel's show with time to spare.

But something else was happening here. He knew it was coming.

Fitzy leaned in close to him. "We've iced three Boko bases and we're pretty sure they have just one more. We also think any Bokos still breathing will try to get out of the country fast. They're not going to hang around after what we've done to their brethren, and we figure they've already got the gas. So hitting that fourth base might be useless. But if we knew for sure where they're escaping to, on what road, and that they didn't have any hostages with them, we could be waiting for them and put an end to this for good and I'll get my wife back."

The big man paused for a moment, choosing his words carefully.

"I hate to ask, Chris," he said finally. "But time is running out and we could use a little help, brother . . ."

Starr asked: "What would you want me to do?" But he already knew what Fitzgerald was going to say.

"Access to a spy satellite would come in handy right now."

Starr really didn't want to hear the actual words. The request was a tall order for many reasons. And there was one big complication: Fitzy didn't realize the U.S. was not supposed to be doing any kind of intelligence gathering when it came to Zuwanda, inside or above it. In fact, there wasn't supposed to be *any* American boots on the ground at all. If Starr ever got caught doing what he was doing, the entire balance of power in Africa and maybe the Middle East would be in serious jeopardy.

"Fitz, you know some mountains are harder to climb than others," he finally told his friend.

But the big man put his hand on Starr's shoulder and looked him in the eyes. He was tearing up; strange to see in such a giant.

"But what if the situation was reversed, Chris?" he asked. "What if Angel was the one being held? And you needed someone's help to get her out?"

Chapter Nine

Starr would commit two federal crimes in the next ninety minutes.

The first felony came via a quick decision. Though his career had been fairly brief so far, Starr knew how America's intelligence agencies worked. His rule of thumb: when in doubt, go right through the looking glass. He never really bought the story that a recalibrating Topaz satellite just happened to capture images of the Hobo camp at Tbango Falls the day before it was obliterated.

More likely, the NRO never stopped its surveillance of Zuwanda. He knew spy techs abhorred disorder and satellites couldn't be turned on and off that easily. If ever asked, it would be easier for them to lie about it than to rewrite and then *reboot* their entire system just because the president of a country the size of Rhode Island didn't want his people to know he was on the take from the United States. Distorting the truth would be so much simpler. Let's not, but say we did.

Or at least Starr hoped that was the case.

He left the truck stop alone, took off in the PAV and used the tomato can to tap into the Topaz-8 constellation.

By dumb luck, one of its eight satellites was due to pass over Zuwanda just ten minutes later.

This one radar satellite could cover the entire country in about two minutes and make its data available in real time. All the person requesting this data needed was the right access code and the right communications device to receive the down link.

Starr had both.

As for breaking into something so highly classified that wasn't supposed to be operating in the first place, Starr wasn't sure what that outcome would be.

The satellite arrived over the country and, as he had guessed, it was still fully operational. From 110 miles high, it beamed down to the tomato can a live moving image that resembled a black and white video but with incredible clarity. It showed every vehicle in transit anywhere on the country's roads.

It was impressive—but it was Topaz's zoom-in capability that made it special. It allowed the viewer to key in on any part of the country, giving them the ability to distinguish trucks from cars, convoys from individual vehicles.

It took Starr no time to spot the fleeing Bokos. Two dozen armed Toyota trucks, moving through the middle of the country, heading north on a little used road called Route 36. There were no hostages with them; that's how sharp the Topaz image was. Starr could see every person in every vehicle and they were all gunmen.

The convoy looked like a snake, making its way through the dark jungle. But about twenty miles behind it, a dull glow was evident in the night. The zoom-in showed a half dozen lorries had been ablaze and were blocking the southern entrance of Route 36. Starr didn't need his pre-cog to know these two events were connected, but he wasn't entirely sure how.

He flew to an intercept point and was soon tailing the convoy from 250 feet up. While enroute, he transmitted all the Topaz-8 information to Bombardment, Inc. That was federal crime number one. Violation of Security Act 623a which prohibited individuals working for U.S. intelligence agencies from giving classified information to unauthorized foreign nationals.

If convicted, it would be life without parole.

The Hobo convoy was trying to reach Uganda under the illusion they might be welcomed there.

Making its way slowly through the night, headlights off, the twelve vehicles were carrying less than a hundred fighters. The last of the Hobos, these men had escaped the three brutal bombardments only because they'd been guarding the Hobo's fourth camp, hidden near a place called Samarro Pass. This was the terrorist army's main camp. This was where their departed leader Bum Hokum used to take his R&R when he wasn't out raiding the countryside.

These men had no hostages with them—not anymore. They had left Samarro with several dozen kidnap victims who'd been made into servants at the main camp. But this was an escape column. Hostages would have slowed them down. So they got rid of them.

The convoy was taking the long route north by design. Route 36 avoided every populated area in the tiny country. But it was even more treacherous than the Kikiwalla, with endless bends and narrower pavements. Navigating it without headlights was a challenge.

It was close to 2:00 a.m. when the driver of the convoy's lead truck checked his smart phone. His GPS app reported they were just ten miles from the border. Word passed down through the convoy and some weary jubilation followed.

Then the sky fell in on them.

It happened at a hairpin turn next to the Ollawagee River. The convoy had to slow to a crawl and the lead truck had to use its headlights; that's how constricted the road was.

But no sooner had the lead truck completed the turn when the convoy was lit by a blinding flash from above.

A rain of mortar shells dropped on top of them just seconds later. They came down in impeccably timed waves, the saturation pattern following the curve perfectly.

The first in line truck was hit exactly three seconds after the second to last. Most of the technicals in between were vaporized in place. The rest became fireballs and plunged into the Ollawagee River below.

Chapter Ten

Starr landed the PAV on the far side of the Ollawagee and climbed up to its southern bluff.

The bombardment truck was there, sitting at the end of a hastily hacked out road a hundred yards across the river from the hairpin turn. Some of the crew was replenishing the truck's ammo supplies—just in case. Others were reattaching its modular side panels. The massive weapon on wheels was being transformed into an ordinary, fairly beat up double tractor truck right before Starr's eyes.

He found Nephew next to the cab of the truck. He was interrogating two young men bound by the hands and feet and sitting on the running board. They were in shock, shaking and disorientated. But they were also two very lucky dudes. They'd seen the massive bombardment up close, yet had somehow lived through it. Truth was, their truck, the last one in the column, had been intentionally spared by the mortar men. Their survival had been by design.

Starr was surprised how young these soldiers were. Both were barely in their teens. Nephew was just completing the interrogation. He walked over to Starr.

"These guys flipped immediately," he told him. "They said they had about fifty hostages with them, but that they dumped them off in the jungle near the beginning of Route 36, at a predetermined place in the jungle."

"Predetermined by who?" Starr asked.

Nephew shook his head. "They're too far down in the food chain to know. But they swear all the hostages they had with them had been freed."

Nephew called up a map of Zuwanda on his smart phone and found the place where the two men said the hostages had been released. Starr was not surprised to see it was the same place where he saw the burning trucks on the Topaz-8 moving file.

He asked Nephew to expand the screen. He pointed to a place not a mile away from the burning trucks.

"That's the National Military Police field headquarters," he told Nephew. "You know, their country club in the middle of the jungle? That might explain the predetermined location those guys told you about."

"Maybe it was one last try by the Hobos to put the squeeze on them and the government," Nephew theorized. "Here's a few hostages, give us some get out of town money?"

"Or they were looking for a free pass," Starr said. "If the fifty freed hostages were transported in those trucks, then burning them was a good way to block Route 36 for a while. Knowing the NMP, there's not much chance of a hot pursuit."

Nephew called out a few orders to his men, checked his watch then told Starr: "Well, there's a good chance those fifty hostages are at the NMP headquarters. We can be there in two hours. Maybe they'll know where the rest of the hostages have been kept all this time. In fact, Fitz is on his way there right now."

Starr was surprised to hear this. "You mean he's not here celebrating this?"

"You missed him," Nephew said. "An NMP border patrol saw our whole thing. Fitzy talked to them afterwards and they agreed to drive him down to their HQ. They said he could wait there and that they'd bring his wife back to him."

Starr was bummed. He wanted to say goodbye to his friend, but he could understand why he went with the national cops. His wife might even be one of the hostages the Hobos just left on the roadside.

Besides, it was time to get back to the OB-16, and catch a ride to Dubai and Angel's big show.

This time he shook hands with Nephew. "Please tell the Irishman that I'll catch up with him soon."

The rest of the mortar team saw what was going on. They stopped what they were doing and on Nephew's signal, snapped to attention and gave Starr a salute.

He saluted back and then was gone.

Down the cliff to the side of the river where he'd hidden the PAV.

Chapter Eleven

Starr was soon airborne again. Climbing to 250 feet, he steered northeast, towards the desert and OB16.

It was mission accomplished. The SEALs could keep their hidden base. The Zuwandans could stop paying blackmail money. The Hobos were gone, no longer a threat to anybody, especially the former hostages. Plus, he'd helped Fitzy finish what he'd set out to do.

And now he'd make it back for Angel's big show.

All's well that ends, his father used to say.

Except . . .

Something didn't feel right.

Every mission has a beginning, middle and end, with a few twists along the way. He'd been involved in enough to know each also has its own timing pattern, its own rhythm.

And this one seemed to end too early—and it was bugging him.

He flew along, trying to understand what he was feeling, but he couldn't put his finger on it. Something was out of order, but that's as far as it got.

Anyone else would just ignore it and go see their model girlfriend do her biggest show ever before an international audience on their seven-month anniversary day.

But that was the problem.

He wasn't like anyone else.

He checked his countdown clock—it was now down to four hours and ticking.

"Sorry, Angel," he whispered.

Then he put the PAV into a long turn and headed south.

He flew for 35 minutes, heart racing, brain cooking, watching the precious time slip away.

At last he spotted the trucks the Hobos had abandoned and set on fire. They were in one long line, six of them, by this time burnt to their bones. He went down to 100 feet and turned up his night vision gear. There were no hostages about; not a surprise. The NMP would have collected them by now and transported them to its country club headquarters nearby.

Case closed.

So why was he here?

He went back up to 250 feet, put the small plane into a sharp turn and headed towards the NMP's HQ.

Almost immediately, his entire body began vibrating. Helmet to boots and back again. He knew what it meant and it was not good. Something was wrong up ahead.

He came over a hill and looked down at the NMP HQ. He'd been expecting to see that little slice of Miami Beach again, just lit up in the nighttime. But he saw no cool lighting, no multi-colored fountains, no flashes of neon.

Instead he saw dozens of harsh sodium lights strung around the corral and the horse barn. What was a beautifully manicured lawn just hours before was now churned up with tire tracks, a strange fog rising from the muddy ground. Every entrance to every building was under heavy guard. A line of military trucks was parked in the shadows near the horse barn. Armed men were everywhere.

Yet he could see no freed hostages, no results of any rescue attempt. Now, his right-lobe forehead began buzzing again. Get ready to be surprised.

He hit a switch on his NVGs and activated the super-ear app. The first sound he heard he thought were horses baying in distress inside the big barn.

But as he drew closer, the sound morphed into something else. It became high-pitched, frantic, alarmed.

Women. Girls.

Screaming . . .

Crying . . .

Begging . . . please, no more.

The hostages . . . They were here. And not just those fifty left at the side of the road. He was hearing *hundreds* of voices. And they all sounded terrified.

He went into another long turn above the place, putting the super-ear into its signals intercept mode allowing him to listen in on any radio traffic coming from below. It only took a minute of eavesdropping for him to learn a horrible truth. A conversation in pidgin English between two officers made several things horrifically clear.

These men knew the last of the Hobos had just been wiped out up near the border. Now they were waiting for their superiors in the capital to decide what to do next. All the hostages *were* here; the officers discussed how they were now stuck with them since the Hobos were all gone. Most telling, the men discussed how the hostages all knew too much about the NMP's relationship with the Hobos. Now that the jihadist gang was no more, the NMP had no one else to blame for the abused condition of the kidnapped victims.

So a mass execution of all five hundred hostages— plus those just released—was being discussed. The hole for a mass grave was already being dug in the fields nearby.

In the meantime, the officers had told their soldiers at the resort, the men who would pull the triggers in such a massacre, that they could plan a mass rape first.

Starr's practice of compartmentalizing his emotions—necessary, the Navy had told him, in order to fully realize his pre-cog abilities—suddenly disappeared in the hot Zuwandan winds.

Everything went red, including his vision, not easy to do while wearing emerald based night vision gear.

No wonder the NMP seemed so impotent when it came to fighting the Hobos. The two sides had made a deal: The terrorists could continue to extort the government. In return, the NMP would hold the hostages and, by the sounds of it, do whatever they wanted to them.

Starr didn't even think about it. He just reached down for the H&K rifle, pulled back the firing bolt and put the PAV into a hair-curling dive.

A quarter-mile long driveway led through some rambling fields and up to the large HQ building; the horse barn was directly behind it. Both had triple the guards watching over them at the moment. The entire estate was on high alert.

Starr leveled off at just 10 feet above the ground and flew right up the driveway. So much noise and commotion was coming from the place, no one heard him approach. He dropped down a couple more feet, the PAV's tail section nearly scraping the ground. Propping up the H&K in the crook of his right arm, he clicked the safety off and raised the rifle up to his NVGs.

The two men standing closest to the front entrance of the horse barn never saw him coming. He pulled hard left, and, like some huge bug, buzzed by them at eye level.

He fired one round into each man's skull and then disappeared back into the night.

Chapter Twelve

Starr committed his second felony once he returned to 250 feet.

This time the violation was against Security Act 624g which forbade U.S. intelligence officers from requesting military action without consent from someone at the Command Level if not higher.

The sin was committed within a one-minute phone conversation with Fong back at OB-16. Starr told the SEAL CO what was happening at the NMP headquarters and then told him what he needed.

Fong never questioned him. He understood right away. He took down all the necessary information and hung up, a willing co-conspirator.

Down below, a phalanx of NMP cops had formed up in front of the huge horse barn, looking in all directions, weapons nervously at the ready. The doors to the barn were closed and padlocked. Somewhere inside were the huddled masses of kidnap victims, 550 of them, plus one, awaiting their fate.

The NMP officers hiding behind the cops could not figure out how their two men had been shot dead. They examined their bodies. Both looked to be hit at close range—but then where was the gunman?

An instant later, it happened again. Two guards at the front door of the HQ itself. One moment alive, the next, their heads shattered.

Then a third time, at the back of the horse barn. Two more men suddenly killed.

The six shootings had happened inside two minutes—and now everyone at the NMP HQ was severely spooked. Not the least of those were the cops who said they'd caught a fleeting glimpse of a flying monster, swooping down out of the night to kill their comrades in such a grisly manner.

It went on like this for almost an hour.

Starr made more than two dozen of the ultra low level strafing runs. He hit his target every time and was so silent on approach, and traveling so fast, he was gone before any of the NMP gunmen were able to get a good shot at him.

They knew something was flying around them, that something was killing them off, one by one. And they shot their weapons at anything that moved, on the ground and in the air. But after sixty minutes and two dozen of their comrades executed, they still didn't know exactly what it was.

In that time, Starr went through three clips in the HK; then two in the .45 automatic. But that was it for his ammunition.

No matter. He started flying dry runs. Low enough and fast enough for all the NMP cops to duck, to throw themselves on the muddy ground, and then shoot blindly into the night sky, lighting it up but missing him by miles.

It was noisy and chaotic, and the random shooting had even started fires in the fields near the mass grave which the NMP cops became obsessed with extinguishing, running around with buckets of sand and hoses used to water the bowling greens.

Starr had succeeded in what he'd set out to do. He'd created confusion in the minds of his enemy. Not enough to win the battle, but just enough to stop them from what they'd been about to do.

It was probably the most dangerous thing he'd ever done, but he didn't care. He'd stopped, or at least postponed a mass rape and maybe a mass murder, and he'd done so by making the NMP thugs deal with some weird monstrous flying bug.

The closest they'd come to hitting him was when someone fired a rifle-launched hand grenade and it exploded right at 250 feet and uncomfortably close by.

When it blew up, all Starr could think was: *Fireworks
. . . again*?

Chapter Thirteen

It was 0400 hours when the two Blackhawk helicopters arrived on the scene.

They came straight down, as if they'd been hiding in the stars.

In seconds, they were hovering right over the horse barn, making a lot of noise and stirring up a lot of dust. Drop lines swirled out of them and the SEALs came sliding down, hurling flash grenades and firing their weapons. Suddenly more than two dozen American boots were on the ground.

Like just about everything the SEALs did, it was over quickly. The firefight with the guards was brief and brutal. A barrage of loud pops! Tap shots in the business. Two dozen guards were all dead, just like that. Many of the NMP officers decided to run, but none of them got far.

The SEALs went through the HQ, clearing the building, floor by floor, employing more flash grenades, using their noise suppressors and their trusty bayonets. The area around the HQ and the horse barn was secure in two minutes. Breaking through the padlocks, a squad of SEALs threw open the barn's doors to be greeted by five hundred weeping, frightened women and girls.

The SEALs immediately began leading the hostages out.

The last group of NMP cops anywhere close by were the ones who'd been fighting the fires in the fields near the bowling greens and who had continued to do so while the gunfight raged about a quarter mile away.

Finally realizing what was going on, they escaped en masse down the hill running towards the jungle.

This was where Squad 2/OB16 was waiting—the flank protection team. The NMP cops ran right into their sights. The SEALs opened up, the NMP cops went down like target dummies, one tap shot a piece.

One last horrible barrage—and then everything was quiet.

Too quiet as it turned out for Starr.

Watching the SEAL attack from the best seat in the house, suddenly he couldn't hear his little electric propeller buzzing any more. That muffled but insistent drone that had been subtly assaulting his ears this whole time was suddenly gone.

His battery had finally run out.

He was going down.

He was able to bank hard left and somehow line himself up with the airport runway next to the smoking NMP

HQ. He was crash landing no matter what; a flat surface would just be the best place to do it.

The problem was he unexpectedly found himself competing for airspace with a trio of giant C-130 Hercules cargo planes. The three aircraft, all wearing night dispersion camouflage, were on their final approach to the same airstrip, just coming in from the opposite direction.

Just barely gliding now, Starr went hard right and passed under the first C-130. He got only a brief glimpse at the big plane, but it was wearing a washed out but visible emblem: East Ghana Air Delivery Service.

They didn't just fly old C-47s.

The Hercules passed over his head a few seconds later, but not by much. Starr somehow rode out three massive waves of heavy prop wash and dropped down, hoping for a haphazard, but semi controlled landing at the far end of the mile long runway. The PAV bounced along the hard surface much longer than it should have, pieces falling off every few feet, its air bags popping and sounding like gun shots.

By the time he stopped moving, the PAV was a jumble of perforated rubber, snapped guy wires and frayed electrical cords. It was totaled. He flashed back to when he took delivery of the little airplane not even a day ago. The label had read: "You are responsible for the contents of this package."

He thought: Will they really take it out of my pay?

He untangled himself from the wreckage, the SEAL body armor saving him from anything more than a few cuts and bruises. His NVG were still working and he looked down to the other end of the runway to see the SEALs were doing a fast-stop procedure.

The big C-130s didn't even turn off their engines. They simply pirouetted 180-degrees, slammed their down back ramps, allowing the SEALs to lead the freed hostages aboard. The quicker they all got out of there, the better.

Starr knew the SEALs were really breaking a lot of commandments here, but not for the first time—or last. That's why they were so good; they were called on to perform irregular jobs all the time. But the orders to engage in such actions usually made their way down from much higher paid grade. Doing all this at the request of a 25-year-old Navy lieutenant?

That was a first.

Starr found Fong near the lead C-130.

He was directing hostages into the airplane, fitting in as many as possible. It would be tight, but none of the hostages was complaining. To their eyes, these soldiers were Americans, and they were here to rescue them. They all went more than willingly.

The Hercules' powerful engines were blowing eve-rything around, people included. Every two or three hos-tages had to hold tight to a SEAL and let him lead them onto the plane safely. It was chaos, but for a change, a good kind.

But Fong's face fell as soon as he saw Starr running towards him.

The SEAL commander told his exec to get the rest of the hostages onto the first plane and then give the pilots the signal to get out of there.

Then he yelled to Starr: "You've got to come with me ..."

They ran past the NMP HQ which was slowly being engulfed in flames, and headed for the horse barn. A few remaining hostages were being led out of the building by Navy commandos.

Fong led Starr into the barn—and for the first time, he saw casualties. About a dozen hostages were badly hurt. Not by the gunfire, but by the brutality rained down on them by the NMP before Starr came flying over the hill.

Fong brought him to a hole at one end of the barn. It had a crude stairway to a chamber below. This was where the Hobos had stashed many of their hostages al-most since the beginning. Starr took just a peek inside the chamber—and that's all he needed. More than 500 people had been jammed into a space the size of a tennis court. It was one of the most horrible places he'd ever seen.

They climbed back out to see the last of the injured were being stabilized enough to be transported to the airplane. But beyond them was a single body, covered by a white sheet. The body was about to be moved by two SEALs; Fong asked them to hang a moment.

He pulled back the sheet.

It was Fitzy.

Starr's heart fell to his feet.

"We found him at the side door," Fong said. "They must have brought him down here, threw him in with the rest of them intending to kill him too. They told us he was protecting some of the hostages from getting assaulted before they shot him. But a lot of people were saved from some high unpleasantness because of what he did."

Starr kneeled before the body and put his hand on his friend's brow. It was already cold.

"Goodbye, brother . . ." he whispered.

The SEALs picked up the body and, along with Fong and Starr, double-timed it to the waiting C-130s.

They ran to the third aircraft. Their cargo bays full of freed hostages, the other two planes were in the process of taking off.

At the bottom of the ramp, Starr saw the last group of hostages being treated by the SEAL team medics. He found Nephew standing nearby. Next to him was a handsome Nigerian woman in her mid-40s.

Starr knew who she was right away.

Damn . . .

Fitzy's wife . . .

The SEALs respectfully carried the body by her and up the ramp, pausing for a moment so she could touch the sheet. Starr didn't know her, but they embraced. Nephew had told her about Starr and what he'd done. She started crying in his arms.

"I feel like I knew him all my life," Starr said to her. "Do you know what I mean?"

"That's the kind of guy he was," she said through her tears.

He took her hands. "All he wanted, every second of every day, was to find you and save you. But because of him—*everyone* got out."

"That his friends accomplished what he started," she said, giving him another hug. "That would make him feel very good."

The last C-130 was ready to take off. All three planes would be transporting the hostages to the large UN relief station at Kisumu in nearby Kenya. They would be reunited with their families from there.

Fong gave Starr a signal, letting him know the SEALs copters were ready to go now.

Starr took out his notebook and a pen. He wrote down his phone number and gave it to Fitzy's wife.

"If you're ever in trouble," he told her. "No matter where in the world you are, call that number and I'll come and get you."

Chapter Fourteen

Angel heard the message she'd been dreading.

"Cinq minutes pour montrer . . ."

Five minutes to show.

She was dressed in Garavani's best outfit; she would be the last model in the first line of twelve on the catwalk. Their audience was overflowing. Paparazzi and the beautiful people were everywhere. The eyes of the fashion world would be focused on her for the next two hours. Twenty outfit changes in all.

Yet Angel's heart was breaking. A big moment about to come and go.

Life . . .

She got one last touch up on her face as a squad of handlers fluffed out the sleeves of her dress. She took her place at the end of the first line of models and told herself to put her mind on what she was about to do. She would be the front cover of every fashion page's media output, around the world, within the hour. Dozens of magazine spreads would follow.

It was time to buck up. Yet, she'd rarely felt so low.

The show began. The first girl did her turn, then the second and the third, on and on. Angel took a deep breath and gave her body a shake.

It was her turn.

The model before her now walked past her as she left the catwalk. She looked Angel in the eyes—and smiled.

This was rare behavior in her business.

Angel walked out, as always the stage lights brighter than she anticipated. She went into her syncopated stroll, each step keeping the beat with the soft chill music pumping from the speakers. The flashes went off; she could hear the crowd softly gasp. They liked her outfit. At least that part went right.

She reached the end of the catwalk, did her turn and began walking back. Against her better judgement, she glanced at table 13B. Her table, in the second row, re-served for her plus one. She'd been peeking out at it be-tween the curtains for the past two hours, only to see it empty. She expected to see the same thing now.

But she was wrong.

Starr was there. He was dressed in soldiers gear— and not ironically. He was muddy and maybe even a little bloody, like he'd just gone through a war.

And he was fast asleep, head down on the table, using his hands as a pillow.

But he was here.

He would later tell her about what happened during the long strange night, including the scramble at the end where he just barely connected with his F-18F taxi ride to get him to Dubai on time.

And it would only be later that he learned the bombardment truck had moved down to the NMP's jungle HQ and after searching it one more time for any innocents, carpet-bombed the place into the ground.

As always, the noise was tremendous—and this time the figure they left in the ground was not a rectangle, but the unmistakable shape of a shamrock. Only those who'd lived through the past few days with them would understand.

Their work complete, Bombardment, Inc. slipped back into the shadows, Zuwanda, all of Africa, and the entire world just a little bit better off because of what they had done.

Coming March 10, 2020

Codename: Starman
Book 2
The Sea of Moons

**Three adventures of Agent Chris Starr,
U.S. Naval Intelligence & Law Enforcement**

**For more information
visit:** www.SpeakingVolumes.us

On Sale Now!

Ben Gannon Deep Sea Thrillers
Books 1 – 3

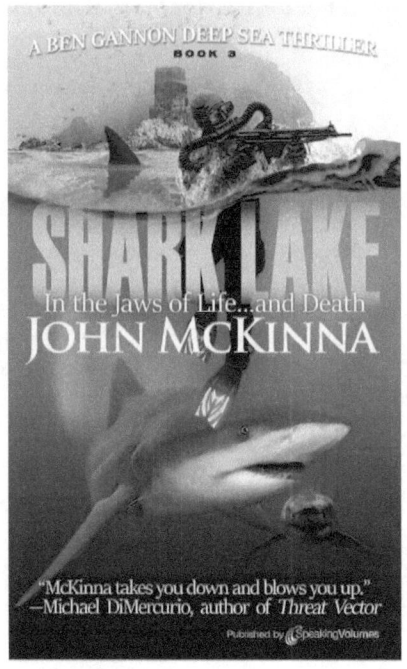

An explosively real novel of underwater action from an author who's been there...

Shark Lake is the newest of the Ben Gannon Deep Sea Thrillers.

For more information
visit: www.SpeakingVolumes.us